To Susan

e   d

on   .

Wd

wishes.

Frank English

30 August 2010

Magic Parcel : The Awakening

Frank English

2QT Limited (Publishing)

First edition published 2010

2QT Limited (Publishing)

Burton In Kendal

Cumbria LA6 1NJ

www.2qt.co.uk

Cover design and Illustrations by

Chaz Wolf

The author has his own website: www.frankenglish.co.uk

Printed in Great Britain by

MPG Books Group, Bodmin and King's Lynn

Mixed Sources

Product group from well-managed
forests, controlled sources and
recycled wood or fiber
www.fsc.org   Cert no. TT-COC-002303
© 1996 Forest Stewardship Council

FSC

A CIP catalogue record for this book is available
from the British Library
ISBN 978-0-9562368-5-2

Dedication

For my wife Denise without whose endless support, patience and understanding this wouldn't have been possible.

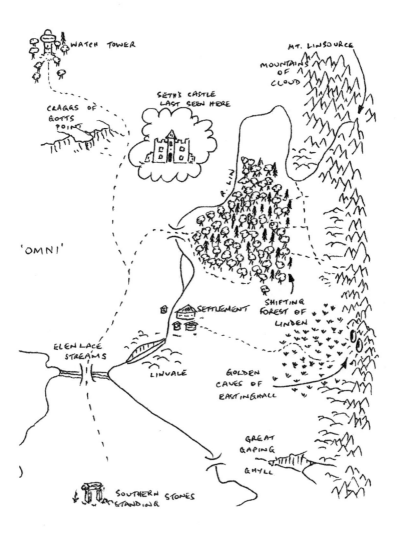

WATCH TOWER

MT. LINSOURCE

MOUNTAINS OF CLOUD

CRAGGS OF GOTTS POINT

SETH'S CASTLE LAST SEEN HERE

A LIN

'OMNI'

SETTLEMENT

SHIFTING FOREST OF LINDEN

ELEN LACE STREAMS

LINVALE

GOLDEN CAVES OF EASTINGHALL

GREAT GAPING GHYLL

SOUTHERN STANDING STONES

Chapter One

There was once a boy, a little boy by the name of Jimmy; Jimmy Scoggins to be exact. He lived with his mother and older brother, Tommy, in a mid-terrace house in an ordinary town in England. They never considered they were anything other than straight forward, regular and the most usual sorts of people.

Although Jimmy was only nine, he was quite a bright little boy for his age. His favourite things of all time were weekends, holidays, and anything which meant he didn't have to go to school. This particular morning, he had to be up early because there was something he badly wanted to do ……

"Jimmy! Jimmy!" yelled Mrs Scoggins in her usual high-pitched, drawn-out wail. "It's half past seven! Time to get up! Jimmeee!"

It's funny how first thing, when you've woken out of a lovely warm dream of that eternal holiday from school, ready to get up for that special visit you've been looking forward to for ages, you decide you don't really want to get up after all. Doesn't that warm blankety feeling make you just wish everyone else would go away?

"I'll just roll over and pretend I didn't hear," thought Jimmy in that semi-drowsy state he called waking up. Why on earth had he wanted to get up anyway? What was so special about *this* particular day?

The thought rang suddenly in his half-empty brain. Covers shot back and he leaped out of his bed - well, crawled anyway - ready for the day. He should have known straight away it was Saturday. There was always a different feel about the morning when it was Saturday, particularly the first Saturday of a holiday. Saturday was always the day he went to see ...

"Uncle Reuben! Why didn't you think of it sooner, idiot," he muttered under his breath, tapping the side of his head with his forefinger; and what's more there was ... "No school! Yippee!"

He hated school even more than cabbage and castor oil - yuck! How he hated school! 'Empty head' is what his class teacher always called him. 'Thoughts in the clouds' he usually said did Mr Bolam. He was all right really, Mr Bolam, Jimmy supposed, in a funny sort of a way. Would have been much better if he hadn't been a teacher, though. Rum lot, those teachers. Always telling you what to do; things they wouldn't dream of doing themselves. Good for you, good for discipline, they always said. Jimmy didn't *not* believe what they said, he just didn't ever listen. Didn't have the time; he was too busy thinking of his next visit to his ...

"Uncle Reuben!" he shouted more clearly as he pulled on his trousers. "Must hurry; can't be late for my bus..." Besides, it was breakfast time, and the smell of bacon frying downstairs was beginning to make him realise his stomach was empty and crying out to be filled.

"Back upstairs," his mum ordered, as he bowled through the kitchen door in his futile attempt to stop himself catapulting into her as she barred the way in, "and put your clean shirt on."

He knew his "Aw, mum!" in complaint, wouldn't cut any ice but he had to try anyway. He turned on his heels and trudged grudgingly back to his room.

"Don't forget to brush your hair and teeth whilst you're at it!" she reminded him as he reached the top step. His attempt to reduce the time he spent at the breakfast table had taken a serious blow. How is it that mothers always seem to know what you are thinking?

"Not much longer to go now, mum," he mumbled at last through two large bulging bags at the sides of his face he called cheeks. He could hardly speak his mouth was so full in a desperate attempt to polish off his breakfast in time to catch his bus. Getting up from the table, he stuffed another bread roll into his groaning cheek sacks - surely they would burst if much more were pushed in. Leaving half his breakfast on his plate for the cat, he made a dash for the door.

"Sit down!" she frowned as he attempted to whiz past her left ear on his way out. "You *will* finish your bacon!"

Jimmy was stopped in his tracks by her commanding voice, and a swift arm-lock applied as his flailing limbs spun past her head. There she goes again, bossing about as usual. Couldn't *he* decide when he had had enough?

"... for your own good," she always nattered. "... ought to do as you are told ... be getting into bother one of these days with not listening ..." she always droned on. He didn't really listen much anyway. Mothers always fussed ... didn't they?

3

"Oh, mum," complained Jimmy. "Can't I just...? I'll miss my bus! Please, mum!"

"Just a little more then, dear," she said quietly, her head drooping slightly to form that stern double chin of finality he knew so well. There was no further use in arguing; that, most definitely, was that. He sat down and began to eat again with as much decent haste as he could, making sure not to stuff too much in at once, or else she would keep him all the more.

"OK," she said quietly again, "that'll do. Off you go now, and don't ..."

She wasn't given the time to finish. He was through into the hallway in a flash, coat and scarf flying behind in his slipstream as he reached the open gate.

She smiled slightly and shook her head in that knowing way all mothers have and to herself she wished him a good time.

Shooting a quick glance to his right as he skidded onto the pavement, he saw the great blue double-decker chugging along the road just a short way lower down. It would be a close run race as to who or what would reach the stop first - bus or boy.

"Oh no!" he panted in full stride, glancing over his flapping scarf; "must ... get ... there! Oh no! I'm going to miss..."

The stop was in sight and he made a last despairing lunge as the bus's bell clanged permission for it to set off, passengers on board. A hand's distance ... not quite ... and then as he was about to miss the darned thing, two great hairy hands appeared from nowhere. Grabbing a hand and the flapping hood of his anorak, the anonymous hands hauled Jimmy towards the platform. Two sensations he felt; one of powered flight, and the other of being almost strangled by his own coat.

Once safely on board, he looked around to find an enormous conductor, who was grinning a great toothless welcome to his number 59.

"Nice of you to drop in," he grinned, bowing low. "Please take a seat. Best views on top. Wipe your feet before you tread on our newly-fitted carpet."

Jimmy mumbled his gratitude and slowly wound his way up the spiral stairway to the upper deck. The bus was one of those ancient carriers which had so obviously been brought out of retirement to fill in for a younger, sprightlier relative which had broken down. It was so old, even the bell wasn't guaranteed to work every time, and even if it did, it was just as likely to ring five minutes after the knob had been pressed, or not at all.

Jimmy shuffled along the side gangway on the top deck between the window and banks of worn bench seats, trying to find somewhere to sit. The big, square, fat or squat frames of the Saturday morning shift at the local foundry works filled the bus, row upon row of silent, unresponsive, reluctant bodies, being taken from the warmth of their weekend laziness.

He eventually managed to squeeze himself into a small space between a fat pair of greasy overalls and a long, thin blue boiler suit, on the front-most seat of the deck, giving him a wonderful view all around. From this seat, which was Jimmy's favourite of all, you could be absolutely *anything*; airline pilot, for example, though he didn't think it would be as cramped as this for space.

"Attention please, this is your captain Jimmy Scoggins calling. I hope you have had a pleasant journey with us. Touchdown will be in ...".

What if an engine caught fire? He could bring her in to land on only one, and be the hero of the day, saving all on board.

Or ... or ... spaceship captain!

"Hello base. Hello base. WIJS calling. Cruising along just below cloud base. No sign of life on this planet as yet, but some strange markings and what appears to be buildings just ahead. Making for them now ..."

And ... and ...

"Tumbles Row; next stop terminus," the harsh voice cut roughly through his inter-galactic adventure, jerking him back to the top deck again. His stop! He hadn't noticed his fellow sardines squeeze out of the can the stop before. He had to hurry along the gangway, down to the platform and out onto the pavement before the bus got up too much speed. On the roadside, panting slightly from his exertions, he gathered his bearings and set off in the direction of his Uncle Reuben's house, a five-minute walk from the stop.

The houses, in the main, had been built between fifty and a hundred years earlier, in their terraced and semi-detached splendour, with long gardens running and tumbling down to neatly trimmed and shaped privet hedges by the path. To Jimmy, they all looked the same, but there was an individuality about each one. If only because of the paintwork outside, each was entirely different from all the others. Immaculate in their appearance and proudly maintained by their owners, they all displayed their best characteristics in the early morning sunshine.

Now, his Uncle Reuben's house *was* different, and rather special. At the end of one of those late Victorian terraces, it stood in a wonderful position in relation to the others in its row. Set in large gardens to three sides, with a strong, high fence all around, the house enjoyed complete seclusion and privacy from prying eyes. To the outsider, it was just another old house and garden, but to Jimmy it was heaven and paradise rolled into one. It was one of those few special places Jimmy could have found with his eyes shut, for whenever he was near to it he had a funny tingling sensation run through and around his body. It was as if he had walked through a very mild electric field, making the hairs on his neck stand on end; not with fear, but with anticipation. For, indeed, he didn't quite know what to expect whenever he visited Uncle Reuben. Something different and exciting always happened.

The garden tumbled backwards and forwards over itself to provide all who entered something different according to his mind and interests. It *was* whatever you *wanted* it to be. There were so many trees and bushes, and so much dense undergrowth that the fence, apart from a few obvious places, could hardly be seen at all. You felt that you weren't even *in* a garden, but somewhere ... up the Amazon, or ... in the Himalayas, or ... or ... even on another planet!

Jimmy hadn't explored it all yet. He hadn't had the time. You see he'd only been going to Uncle Reuben's every Saturday since he was six, and now he was nine. There was always the odd corner he seemed to have missed, or *that* particular area he was sure wasn't there the last time, or *that* rather interesting-looking old shed he hadn't noticed. Always something...

There was that tingling feeling again! He was almost there. One more corner, and ... Uncle Reuben, as always, standing on the front step (the top one of ten to be exact), thumbs under lapels, and boot caps flashing as he smiled his welcome to his favourite nephew. In the years he had known him, Jimmy had never seen that smile leave his face. He was one of life's optimists; he saw good in everything, and had a great deal of wisdom and 'extra' knowledge that other people didn't have.

He was a funny old soul really, if you stopped to think; shortish, quite thickset, with a great bush of black, curly hair which always stayed in the same position but never seemed orderly or to have been combed. And those horn-rimmed, half-moon spectacles he had perched permanently, like a bird ready for take-off, on the end of his nose, added a certain odd look to him, like some absent-minded professor. Absent-minded he certainly was not. Jimmy was forever puzzled how he knew so much (he always had an answer for all, absolutely *all*, of Jimmy's questions), and he never seemed to forget anything you told him, no matter how long ago it was. Although he swore he could not see an inch without them, Uncle Reuben never seemed to look *through* those glasses, but usually *over* them. And those eyes - they were so sharp, bright and deep that you couldn't imagine them, ever needing glasses.

He didn't know very much about Uncle Reuben, except that he had always been there – well, ever since his father had died when he was five. Reuben had taken over responsibility for the education and wellbeing of both Jimmy and his brother, Tommy, who was now thirteen. Mother had shown Jimmy photographs of his uncle from years and years ago, from long before he had been born. The funny thing about him was that he never looked any different. He had remained the same 'age' for the last twenty or thirty years at least; but that was impossible.

Was it though? Jimmy had begun to wonder, especially since he had come to know him over the years.

"Hello Jim, old chap," Reuben greeted his nephew as he rushed through the gate, which always closed itself, and down the path. Jim was his preferred name, not the 'Jimmy' his mother insisted calling him, nor the 'James' he so often was called at school. As with so many things, Reuben always knew what you were thinking and what your wishes were. He also treated you, not as a little boy, but as an adult, an equal.

"Hello, uncle," Jimmy replied, "sorry I'm a bit late, but the bus was slow and I nearly missed my stop."

"That galactic mission, eh?" Reuben asked, bushy eyebrows becoming almost lost in that black mop as they slowly crept up his forehead, and eyes twinkling above the rim of his spectacles. "Any way, come on in. Coffee's in the pot, and your favourite ice cream is on the kitchen table."

Jimmy had stopped questioning how Reuben knew what he was thinking, and how he had discovered what his favourite ice cream flavour was for that week (he changed it so often); he now just accepted that's the way it was. He had even changed his choice of flavour on the bus that morning so only he knew his favourite; but to no avail. There it was, on the table when he got there, the flavour he had chosen! He was a marvel, that uncle was; the sort *every* boy should have.

"You know that story you were telling me the last time I was here?" Jimmy mumbled through a mouthful of walnut and coffee ice cream, his new favourite. "You know, the one about the other world - the one through the fence."

"Yes, old man," Reuben answered, eyes glinting over his glasses. "Yes, I do."

"Well," Jimmy went on. "You didn't tell me what happened. Could we finish it today, please? I've tried to think of ways the Chieftain might get his country back, but I'm sure I've no idea."

My, that ice cream was good. He wasn't sure which he liked best - the ice cream or the stories. If only school was like this - he would stay there during the holidays! It was strange that the ice cream dish *always* stayed full until you had had enough, and only then did it empty. No, really, the stories were the best; foreign countries, other worlds, space travel, people. Reuben knew how to keep little boys interested forever.

"OK then," Reuben grinned. Let's go into the lounge and see where we were."

The lounge was one of those enormously high rooms so popular about a hundred years earlier, with a large decorated fireplace and a long, curved wooden mantle piece over the fire grate. It never changed. The décor always had that freshly painted look, as if the decorators had only just packed away their pots, brushes and covers, and walked out the door just before *he* had walked in. The late morning sun stole through the slats of one fawn-coloured, half-closed shutter as they settled in front of a crackling fire in the black-leaded grate. They sat with a large glass of orange juice on their knees.

"Before we start, Uncle Reuben," Jimmy said, fixing his relative's glinting half-moons, "one thing has been puzzling me since the last time."

"Yes, old chap," Reuben asked, "and what is that?"

"Well," he went on, "I've been looking at some old

photographs Mum gave me, and ... and ... why do you look the same? I mean ... why don't you look older now?"

Reuben's eyes wrinkled at the corners as his brows met in the middle and threatened to cover his eyes altogether. That same smile played around his mouth, which widened slightly to reveal two rows of even, white teeth.

"I'll let you in on a secret," he confided, bending closer to Jimmy as he dropped his voice to a whisper. "A secret I've never told anyone else yet."

Jimmy's eyes widened, eager to learn anything about this remarkable man, particularly anything *nobody else* knew. His mouth opened slightly, and his cheeks grew vaguely pink as he almost stopped breathing in anticipation of what he might hear.

"You see," he went on, "I'm at least three hundred and fifty years old, and I've been on other worlds different from this one as well."

The light grew steadily dimmer in the room and all noise gradually faded away until all Jimmy could hear was the gentle hiss of complete silence. And all he could see was the glowing face of his uncle, not a hand's width from his own face.

"I don't age very quickly," Reuben added, "so you wouldn't tell any difference if you were to see me a hundred years from now. Yes, I shall still be here in a hundred years time. You see, I'm ..."

There was a loud bang at the front door which made Jimmy jump almost onto the mantelpiece. He blinked his eyes, that slow blink as if waking from a long sleep and interesting dream, and found the room flooded with light again; and his uncle no longer there. He waited for a few minutes and, as Reuben didn't return, he decided to explore the garden to pass the time.

"Must have been somebody important," he muttered as he stepped out of the scullery door into the brilliant late morning sunshine. Standing on the top step and surveying the scene before deciding where to go first, he noticed that the garden was an entirely different lay out from that he had seen the week before. Down towards the bottom of the long herbaceous border where there had been a great bank of thick leathery laurel bushes, there was now a wide gap, showing the sturdy fence beyond; and surely that shed ... had become much ... bigger?

Puzzled, he set off down the stone steps and climbed across the turned stone balustrade at the bottom, to strike out across the well-manicured lawn. Usually he didn't manage to reach the end of the garden, for interesting objects often caught his eye en route, off to the left or right. This time, however, there was no distraction; no deviation.

Reaching the end of the lawn, he stepped out onto the wide gravel path which led across the border to the fence. With only two strides crunched along its noisy way, he stopped, realising that the path he now took for granted, should not have been here at all. And the space he had just walked through should have been an enormous weeping willow! The fence, however, seemed to draw him, against his will almost; tall, black, sinister, letting through no chink of light from beyond, it pulled Jimmy ever closer.

In the gloom, underneath its shadow, he peered as you would through the doorway into a dark room, trying to see more closely. Suddenly, off to his right, he caught sight of something glowing slightly, about halfway up the oak staves. He blinked and strained his eyes again trying to make out what it was.

"Funny," he muttered, "that wasn't there before. What is it?"

He moved closer, entering the shadow completely.

"Can't be!" he whispered to himself, though he didn't know why. There was no-one thereabouts to overhear him. "It's a ... a handle!"

Sure enough, there was the faint, silvery, ghostly outline of a curved, knobbed door handle in the fence, but no door could he find.

"Who on earth would want to put a door handle in a fence?" he puzzled, half-smiling, half-nervous. "I wonder if ..."

He reached out to touch the handle, but changed his mind halfway, only to find his hand drawn, involuntarily, towards the object of his attention. The silvery, transparent outline became solid as his fist closed around its metal exterior. He found himself putting his weight against the lever in an effort to open up whatever was beyond.

The handle was fully depressed when a small door-shaped section of the fence moved slowly inward towards the waiting boy. A grey mist began to form and to creep out from beyond, flowing along the ground towards him, as a profound silence fell over everything.

"Jim! Jim!" a deep clear voice, like a spring morning after a night of rain, rang out from the house, breaking the spell around him. "Lunch is ready!"

Jimmy spun around, loosing his grasp on the latch, and

caught sight of his Uncle Reuben's unmistakable form at the bottom of the house steps. He waved, but turned once again to find that the handle was no longer there, the fence was simply a fence. And the whole area was flooded in warm sunlight the like of which he had never felt before.

Chapter Two

"Uncle?" Jimmy's muffled voice struggled through a large mouthful of his favourite apple pie and ice cream.

"Yes, old man," Reuben's smile spread even further, "what do you want to know?" He knew that whenever the lad used his name in that slow, puzzled, questioning tone, there was some insoluble problem bothering his mind. He never disappointed the boy, always answering every question with equal care.

"Why was there a handle in the fence at the bottom of the garden?" Jimmy asked, his face lifting upwards towards his uncle.

"Ah," was the soft reply, as a new knowing look took over Reuben's eyes. "You've seen it then?" His tone conveyed the feeling that there was an air of inevitability about it - that Jimmy would have found 'it' sooner or later.

"What would have happened if I had opened the door?" Jimmy insisted. "Where did it lead to? There was a bit of mist and a lot of darkness, and ..."

"Come through into my study," Reuben suggested, noticing the boy had finished his second helping of pie. "We can talk better there without interruption."

"But, there's no st...", Jimmy half-protested, somewhat puzzled at the suggestion.

"There are 'others' who may hear," Reuben whispered,

the smile almost disappearing from his face as he crossed his lips with his forefinger.

Jimmy's eyes widened and his mouth opened to a small circle as if he was about to suck invisible lemonade up through a transparent straw. Nothing further was said until they reached that most important of places Jimmy never knew existed let alone had seen - Reuben's study.

As they walked along the familiar thickly carpeted hallway towards the front door, uncle followed by nephew. Jimmy became even more confused, and was about to ask Reuben why they were going out, when, suddenly, there it was, to their right. *That* door certainly had *not* been there before. Jimmy was definite about that. It stood amidst shadow, slightly recessed from the rest of the wall, forming a small, square lobby in which somebody could stand quite comfortably and not be seen.

A deep and brooding silence had fallen over the house, so that even the ticking of the kitchen clock could be heard quite distinctly. As they approached the door, Jimmy tried to moisten his dry lips by his even drier tongue. The tiny hairs on the top of his back and base of his neck began to prickle with more than a little fear and apprehension, even though Reuben was there.

As they neared it, the door became much clearer; dark oak staves fitting closely together to form a thick barrier. Where had he seen that before? The fence! Yes, of course! It matched exactly the fence at the bottom of the garden, except that here there was neither handle nor knob, nor any visible means of entering.

Reuben stepped forward, closed his eyes and began to

whistle softly, almost inaudibly, whilst passing both hands lightly over the smooth surface of the door. After a few moments, it began to move inwards; slowly at first, and then suddenly they were in, door fast shut behind them.

Jimmy simply stood where he was, unable to move for what he saw around him. Eyes wide with surprise, wonder and excitement, he let his gaze amble around the room, flitting from object to object, quite unable to believe what lay before him.

Large by the standards of his own home, the room was dominated by an enormous, dark, polished oak desk, carved around with intertwining leaves, stems and faces of animals he did not recognise. The green leather inset top of the desk was clear except for one object - a large blue and green geographical globe set on a golden stand. The countries traced on that globe, however, bore no resemblance to any Jimmy knew of. In fact, they were not countries which were to be found anywhere in his world.

The walls were half-covered in the most beautiful red rosewood panelling, which was inset with shelf upon shelf of books of all shapes and sizes; leather-bound, or paper-cased, all were well-thumbed as if in continual use. Many of the titles were in foreign languages he didn't understand, and the others were in an English, which might as well have been foreign for what sense they made to him.

Although he wanted to look at everything, he couldn't keep his gaze from being drawn to the most remarkable feature in the room. The walls above the panelling were hung with great sheets of shiny cloth upon which were printed maps of many different countries, some of which were flattened-out versions of countries on the globe.

Others, however, were obviously not of *that* world either, and on closer examination, he discovered that the details on the maps had been picked out in different coloured embroidery silks and were not in printing ink at all. Between the maps, giving further details of the countries, there were dozens of drawings on stiff card. They were of many items; from places to exotic animals to people dressed in strange clothes, clearly not of this land. He must have spent ten minutes in silent amazement before he realised that Uncle Reuben had been watching him all the time, face wrinkled in that irrepressible grin.

"Wow!" was the only sound he could utter at first, when the trance had worn off. "Where *are* these places? We do a lot of geography at school, but I never saw these places in any of our geography books. Mind you, they're pretty old. Can't afford any more, Mr Bolam says, and ..."

"They are not on *this* world," Reuben interrupted slowly, quite deliberately waiting to see Jimmy's reaction.

As if half-expecting that answer, Jimmy's voice continued to ramble on but gradually it slowed and tailed away to a complete silence, rather like one of those old gramophone machines running down. He stood for a moment or two, hands by his sides, looking into those deep, wise eyes of his Uncle Reuben, whose face had not changed one bit. Reuben took hold of Jimmy's hand in one of his own, which, compared with the rest of his body, was incongruously large. With a slight nod of the head, he led him towards the largest map of all, directly behind the desk. As they approached, the great flag-like map began to descend until it was the right height for a small boy to see. The roundness of his eyes betrayed the wonder he experienced as he examined the country more closely.

Bordered with the same intertwining leaves and flower stems as the great desk, there were hundreds of little pictures illustrating the different areas of the land - from mountain to river; from castle to village; from wild craggy sea's edge to soft flowing countryside, meadow and wood. All were so real, and the detail so finely picked out, the figures might have been ready to jump out into the room.

As Jimmy was watching the story of the land play before him, he was at first unaware of the almost imperceptible and melodic drone of his uncle's voice as it told of the land unfurling before his eyes. Consciously unaware he might have been, but subconsciously his mind took in every detail, every word, every description.

"Omni is the land you see before you," Reuben started. "It is the country which is everywhere, and nowhere. Like many others, and yet different, it is wherever you want it to be. The people you see are the same as those in your own world but you may not recognise them as such. All the worlds you see on these walls are the same but set in different times and surroundings and ..."

Jimmy *thought* he understood what Reuben was talking about but for the most part he just stood and watched as the stories Reuben told brought to life the pictures before him. The stories went on and on, and took him further into different worlds. If it hadn't been for the panelling in front of him and desk's edge pressing into his back, he would have been there amongst the trees and animals, feeling the wind on his skin, and swallowing in great gulps the salty tang of the seaward breeze.

Lunchtime had turned into mid-afternoon before Jimmy

realised that the uplifting voice of his uncle had stopped, letting him down gently from its pinnacles of excitement to the carpet of the lounge. The study had somehow slid away leaving him wondering if...

His uncle, by this time, was standing next to him, hand around his shoulder, and with a small brown-paper parcel under the other arm.

"Time's getting on, old man," Reuben started, eyes dancing like the sparkle of light on a flowing river; "and I had clean forgotten that this parcel must be posted today. Post Office shuts in half an hour, and I was wondering...?"

"I'll take it uncle," Jimmy butted in eagerly.

"I rather hoped you would," his uncle replied with a broadening smile. "The stamps are on, so here's some money to call in at Mrs Timberley's shop to get yourself some of those caramel toffees you like."

"Great! Thanks uncle," Jimmy grinned as he skipped down the front steps, parcel tucked underneath his arm.

"Have fun, and don't forget to be back for tea!" Reuben's voice bounced down the path after him as Jimmy skipped through the gate and onto the pavement. He almost knocked over an old man, muffled in a grey overcoat and scarf even though it wasn't particularly cold; but he had no hat on to protect his shiny, bald, grey-rimmed head from the breeze.

"Hang on, boy!" he exclaimed in a curiously thin, reedy voice, rather like someone blowing across the edge of a taut blade of grass. "Careful now! Eh? It's young Scoggins, isn't it?"

"Yes," Jimmy replied, apologising as he picked up the old man's umbrella from the gutter he had knocked it into. "Sorry, Mr Grainger, I didn't see you."

Mr Grainger was a strange old man who lived across the road from his uncle. He had a tiny little wife who hardly ever spoke, and a small wire-haired terrier, which seemed to have two of its feet in the grave. His house had a neat little garden, complete with pond and fishing gnomes at the front, and miniature flowers and things at the back. He was often to be seen and heard shouting at the local lads for kicking their footballs over his rather small wall and fence. He had, on more than one occasion, threatened to call the police, but of course he never did. Grumblin' Grainger the boys called him, not to his face of course, but they pulled faces behind his back, which wasn't very polite. He had a large stock of confiscated footballs of all shapes and sizes, which he swore he would return one day. But the trouble was, he had had some of those balls for fifteen years or more, and their owners wouldn't necessarily want them returned - if he could remember whose they were!

He had a shed - a very nice potting shed - at the bottom of his garden where he spent most of his time, pottering about in the summer and spring, and snoozing in the colder months. He had a huge cast iron stove in that shed, which took up about a quarter of the available space inside. It had an enormous black pipe poking out of the shed's roof, belching out thick yellow smoke from its top. Everybody in the neighbourhood complained and tried to get him to take it down because it spoiled the look of the area (not to mention the smoke!), but he kept it and carried on in his own cantankerous way. His wife didn't seem to have much sway over his activities either, choosing to let him go his own sweet way to save arguments (anything for a quiet life, she always said).

"Now then, young Scoggins," Mr Grainger went on, "are you behaving yourself?"

'Oh my God, here he goes again', Jimmy thought groaning inwardly; 'same old questions, same old conversation'. "Yes, Mr Grainger," he replied politely, when in fact he wanted to say 'mind your own business'. This was an exact replay of every occasion in the past when he had been confronted by Grumblin' Grainger, who didn't seem to know how to talk to people other than to complain.

"'Ello, 'ello, 'ello," came a deep rumble from just behind them, rescuing Jimmy from a long, drawn-out history of how good children were in Mr Grainger's day. It was PC Jamieson, an amiable and rather large policeman from the local station.

"Hello, PC Jamieson," Jimmy said, smiling broadly and heaving a huge sigh of relief. The policeman recognised Jimmy's relief and, winking, offered to walk along with them.

He was a well-liked man, was PC Jamieson, particularly by the children of all ages in the neighbourhood. He was the sort who would tell you off after a complaint from an adult but not before giving you a private behind-the-back wink and afterwards a don't-worry-too-much grin. Not that PC Jamieson didn't tell people off in earnest - he did, but only when he considered you had done something really wrong or worth telling you off for. Consequently he stood no nonsense, and everyone respected him for it.

"Well, Jim," the policeman went on, a big grin spreading half way across his face, "holiday again next week, eh? Tell you what, if you want to come to visit your uncle in the week, I'll take you up to have a look around the station. How's that?"

"Would you really?" Jimmy said, a look of excitement crossing his face at the prospect. "That would be excellent."

"Make it Wednesday," the PC went on, tossing his head back as if ready to let out one of his great guffaws of pleasure, "and I'll pick you up here. Can't stop now, so I'll see you then. Bye for now, and mind how you go."

He turned away from Jimmy and Mr Grainger, who through all of that had been strangely silent, and took his enormous frame down the next side road where he had parked his bike. The last Jimmy saw of him was his great body, black cape flying out behind in the breeze, on top of that black regulation police bicycle, rounding the next corner down.

As soon as the PC was out of sight, Grumblin' Grainger started up again exactly where he had left off, into the same long history of childhood behaviour he had given out, on many occasions before. Jimmy groaned inwardly again, and his head began to shrink into his anorak hood, which he had put on to escape the incessant drone of his earnest companion. He clutched his uncle's parcel even more tightly under his arm, as they headed, at Mr Grainger's snail pace, towards the post office.

Unfortunately for Jimmy, he would have to share his journey all the way because it was pension day for Mr Grainger, and that meant *post office*.

"Oh dear! Oh dear!" thought Jimmy. "I *wish* I hadn't bumped into Mr Grainger. I *wish* I was on my own. I wish ... I wish ... like anything I was in ... in ... ***Omni!***"

24

Thoughts of the country he shared with his uncle - that beautiful, unexpected, far off place - flooded his mind as he clamped his eyelids fast shut in his attempt to escape. For a second nothing happened and all was still, and then thousands of tiny white dots started dashing about on a black velvet backdrop in his head as his eye lids squeezed together even tighter, as if by order. Quickly the white dots grew until there was something, which rather resembled a dense snow blizzard, or a television screen when the aerial's not right or tuning's not on station.

He tried several times to open his eyes again, feeling like someone who had walked into a feather pillow factory and couldn't find the exit, but he couldn't; they were tight shut. Now, feeling that this state of affairs - being unable to open one's own eyes - was not quite as it should be, he began to get just a little afraid that his eye lid motors had jammed or something, when he was suddenly thrust out into the open again. His eyes automatically squinted as the glare of the brilliant sun hit him across his face, making him feel rather like a person coming from a darkened room into intense light.

It took his vision several minutes to accustom itself to the glare, and when it did, Jimmy could do nothing but stand as he was, and stare in utter disbelief and astonishment. To his intense relief, Grumblin' Grainger had disappeared (which could only have been a blessing), but so had everything else - no road, no terraces, no cars - only trees, grass, and ... that enormous red sun!

He blinked. He blinked again, harder this time, and rubbed his eyes, almost dropping the parcel, forgetting it was still under his arm.

"This isn't Victoria Road," he observed, his voice ringing out in the clear, clean air of the countryside, with nothing to stop or drown it. He clapped his hand to his mouth, taken aback by the loudness of his words, even though he had intended it simply as a mumble. The sweat was by now beginning to collect on his forehead in small beads, and the rest of his body felt sticky and hot under his quilty anorak, as the sun's heat bore down on him, trying to press him in to the ground.

He put down the parcel between his feet, so he would not lose it, and took off his coat before he melted and, fastening it around his waist by its arms, he turned completely around, scanning the area he found himself in.

An uneasy, panicky feeling started to creep up inside; that feeling you get when you realise you are lost in a place you don't know, and, much as you look around for a friendly face, you don't find one. He was entirely alone, with only the trees and birds for company.

Mr Grainger received many rather strange looks from passers-by as he maintained his continuous stream of advice and comment to his audience. It wasn't until he had almost reached the post office that he stopped for breath and turned towards his young listener to find he was ... alone!

"Well, blast me! The little b...," he gasped, face colouring to a bright crimson. "He's taken himself off!" His voice became squeakier than ever, and a slight wheeze could be heard rattling in his throat as his temperature soared, and he threatened to explode.

He did manage to calm down, however, shortly after a

young woman stopped and asked if he was all right. He shambled off, threatening dark things to that young rascal when he saw him again.

Chapter Three

As the clock hands drew on to six o'clock in the evening - Jimmy's usual return time - and past, his mother became increasingly agitated.

Half past six had arrived, then hastily departed, and she could stand it no longer. She was convinced he had had an accident, been spirited away, or, even worse, missed the bus. When it got to seven o'clock, and the first heralds of dusk were stealing in and paving the way for the dark armies of night, she was convinced that the worst had happened.

"Oh, that dratted boy!" she muttered to herself as she tidied the kitchen for the third time. "Where on earth can he be? He ought to consider my feelings, making me worry like this."

This was her way. Concerned underneath all, but not showing it outwardly too much.

"Tommy," she shouted finally, unable to contain herself. "Tom..."

"Yes, mum," he answered from close behind her left ear.

"Oh dear!" she blurted out, throwing her head into the air and almost jumping over the table. "Don't creep up on me like that! Listen," she went on, "Jimmy's not come back from Uncle Reuben's yet. Would you catch the half past seven bus and see where he is?"

"Why don't you phone?" Tommy replied, reluctant to leave his favourite TV show.

"You know very well," she frowned, "that Uncle Reuben doesn't hold with telephones. Says they ruin conversations. You can't tell who's at the other end anyway."

"OK mum," Tommy offered over his shoulder as he was leaving the room. "I'll get my coat and be off then," and with that he was gone.

The journey might have been an exact replay of Jimmy's earlier that day; same old substitute bus was just pulling away; Tommy was hauled on by the same tuneful, mountainous conductor; he felt the same tingle and twinge as he approached his uncle's house. This time, though, Reuben, as if expecting Tommy to call at that precise moment, was waiting at the gate, usual grin across his welcoming face.

"Well now Tom," he said, holding out his hand in greeting. "Nice to see you. Haven't been around here for quite some time, have you?" He paused to look at Tommy over his glasses, with as near a reproachful gaze above a cheery smile as you would ever come near to seeing from him.

"Mum's worried," Tommy said in a quiet voice as they wandered up the path towards the house.

"Ah, yes," Uncle Reuben smiled, eyes twinkling knowingly.

"She's asked me to see where Jimmy is," Tommy continued, and as he spoke a slight smile began to play around the corners of his mouth, and, as he read the face of his uncle, it grew slowly into a great grin of understanding.

"I think you know where he's gone, don't you?" Reuben said, eyebrows threatening to engulf his glasses, once they were in the lounge.

"The parcel?" Tommy asked, answered almost before he spoke by a gentle nodding from Reuben.

"... and the same place as I ...?" Tommy went on.

"Yes, indeed," Reuben continued. "The same as you visited. I thought he needed a little adventure, don't you know. So I gave him the Parcel to post. He should be there by now. Would you like to go through to see that he misses nothing?"

"Yes please," Tommy said, eyes beginning to sparkle again at the thought. "I think so and ..."

"Well, you'll have to be sharp," Reuben interrupted. "Light's going quickly and I can keep the way open for only a short while longer. Down to the bottom of the garden now, and look for the handle in the fence you saw a long time ago. Turn it and go through. The rest is up to you."

Here he stopped short and gave Tommy one of his quizzical, piercing looks again, *through* his glasses this time to see if he really meant business. Satisfied he did, he sent him off with his blessing, and with one piece of advice ringing in his ears.

"Look beyond what you see," he advised. "Don't take anything at face value, and above all accept help when it's least expected."

The last sentence floated down to him as he headed for the bottom of the garden, and was the last thing he heard. As he approached the bottom fence, invisible in the heavy shade, a strange feeling of fullness and expectancy crept over him, cutting out all outside noise and enveloping him in a deadening blanket of silence. It was as if he had walked into a thick wall of foam. The fence he could now see as if someone had obligingly turned on a dim light, creating eerie half-shadows around the shrubs and bushes. To him in this light, the vertical staves seemed to form a solid wall of wood, when there, below right, he caught sight of the handle he had used so many times before, glowing faintly in the gloom as if it had been painted onto the wood.

As his fingers closed to take hold, it became solid in his hand, yielding under his determined pressure. A faint crack appeared around the outline of the door as Tommy pulled the handle towards him, and as the crack grew, brilliant sunshine poured through, flooding the border he was standing on with golden red light. He stepped back two paces to allow the door to swing wide on its unseen hinges, and in doing so he took a deep breath and launched himself into the new world. As his trailing foot crossed the line and trod earth on the other side, the door closed silently behind him, leaving no trace at all. He was surrounded by countryside, trees and a warmth so overwhelming he could have laid down to sleep where he stood.

A tingling of excitement swept over the boy as he surveyed the already well-known scene; the same excitement he had experienced on numerous other occasions; no panic, no apprehension, no fear. The wonderful and fortunate thing about 'handle-hopping', as he called it, was that you were always guaranteed to land in exactly the same place. You couldn't always guarantee when the handle would appear in Reuben's garden, but once through, you were sure of where you were. He had been here only once with the parcel - the first time, and every other time through the door in the fence. He had no idea, however, where his brother had ended up. Parcel travel was so imprecise and inaccurate. Each time it was used by successive travellers, it took them to different places. He would have to enlist help he could see that.

"Oh well," Tommy said, taking a deep breath again and moving forward, "here goes. Standing about will not do a jot of good. Think I'll see if I can find my old friend Tarna. He'll know where to look."

"There's no need," a deeply resonant voice split the quiet air just behind Tommy. "I am here."

Tommy spun round on his heels, startled by the unexpected presence. He screwed his eyes up for a moment in concentrated thought, trying to recognise ...

"Tarna! My old friend! But ... I ..." Tommy stuttered. "How ...?"

"Do not forget," the newcomer answered, a great grin splitting his dusky face, "that in Omni, whatever you wish is, and that whatever you want to be, can become reality. It is a long time since you were last here," he continued, casting a reproving eye towards his companion. "Had you forgotten your old friends?"

"Well, er, no really," Tommy answered uncomfortably, for really he *had* forgotten about the excitement of the other world. In fact, he had begun to think it was all just a little - dare he admit it - babyish for him now that he was thirteen. Tarna's eyes twinkled, an almost imperceptible smile creasing the corners of his mouth. He understood, although he and others like him didn't share such other-world feelings. He determined to himself from then on that he would reintroduce Tommy to the excitements they once shared, the adventure of the country, and would help him to rediscover their old haunts.

Suddenly, as they were talking, the red sun went out and a chill shadow spread over them, destroying the caressing, welcoming warmth with an uninvitingly cold shudder. The smile drained slowly from Tarna's mouth as he raised his face towards the offending intruder.

He screwed up his eyes, and pulled his collar around his chin as his mouth began to move, uttering silent and bodiless words. The cloud disappeared as suddenly as it had formed; dispersed, it seemed, by some unfelt and unheard wind. As the sun poured over his face again, Tarna opened his eyes, but his smile remained hidden behind a disturbed and troubled look.

"Why do you look so worried?" asked Tommy, puzzled.

"Sarni, the eclipsing cloud," Tarna went on, "appears only at times of great hardship, disaster or unrest, and for it to disappear so soon can only mean ..."

He was interrupted by a long piercing, drawn-out wail the like of which Tommy had never experienced before, sending shivers of fear down his back.

"What in heaven's name was that?" Tommy asked, as he felt the hairs on the back of his neck bristle and the goose pimples on his bare flesh begin to march up his arm.

"We cannot stop here to speak," Tarna answered. "We must away to my village. That is an evil omen indeed. The Senti are abroad again."

"Senti?" puzzled Tommy. "What are they?"

"Sorry, yes," Tarna said in a low voice. "They weren't here when you started coming. They are the Sesqui-senti,

33

servants of the evil Lord Seth. Their white, eyeless forms are sent by their master to do his bidding. That they are abroad searching for food is bad news and ..."

"Yes," Tommy replied a little impatiently, "but what *are* they, and who is Seth?"

"Whether bred or made, I know not," Tarna went on, "but they home onto warm-blooded creatures as if by magic. As for Seth, he is a wicked, evil magician who is able to make his castle disappear and reappear anywhere at will. He and his evil brood haven't been seen for a very long time, since before your time, when he swore he would conquer the world and become its master. So far, fortunately, he hasn't been able to fulfil that aim."

"Well," Tommy interrupted, "if he's so powerful and so clever, how come he hasn't taken over before now?"

"There is a power in the land," Tarna said, "older and far greater than Seth. The Keeper of that power - or he may even be the power itself, we do not know - is a great magician, whose strength still has the measure of Seth's wizardry; for the time being. His name to us is Algan, the Binder. He is rarely seen save in time of great need, but without his presence, Omni would soon be overcome by darkness. He lives somewhere out there ..." He paused to wave an indecisive arm in a general northerly direction. "But we do not know where. No one has ever seen his stronghold or even knows that it is, in fact, *there* at all."

This puzzled Tommy, for his mind shot back to that first glimpse of the map of Omni he had in his uncle's study - the same one seen by Jimmy - and there on the map, to the north-west, wasn't that Algan's cave and forest marked? Surely!?

"Surely ..." Tommy started again, but wasn't allowed to

finish. He found a large hand clapped over his mouth, and himself being thrown unceremoniously into a nearby thicket of bushes. Tarna kept his hand over Tommy's mouth until he was sure he understood not to speak. Then, creeping to a small chink in the branch tangle, he beckoned to his companion, and, whispering in his ear and pointing outwards, he indicated an area he wanted him to see.

"Look," he hissed almost inaudibly, "down the path, to the right a little, close to that yew. Do you see it? There's a slight grey mist forming around the tree - there it is again, clearer this time!"

Tommy peered intently in the direction his host indicated, and eventually saw what Tarna had become so agitated about; a short form biped, dressed all over in close-fitting grey - or could it have been skin? It stood there, swaying to and fro, as if ... sniffing the air, the head swivelling in a horizontal semi-circle, trying to find ... its ... direction? The neck stiffened suddenly and all movement ceased. Without warning, the same tearing screech as before broke from its sightless face, taking both Tommy and Tarna by surprise. But this time they noticed a change in its tone. There was a message there, one of almost triumph. Soon other Senti appeared as if from nowhere, homing in on their companion's call. Tommy flung himself backwards, realising with horror that their corporate movement forward was on a direct line to their hiding place. His eyes rolled helplessly in fear, and as he looked into the face of certain capture, he could hear that dry, rattling shuffle, as if a winter breeze was chasing along a pile of long-dead and dry beech leaves.

Tarna, realising almost too late why they had been

35

singled out, well hidden though they were, threw himself onto his friend, shielding him from the advancing bloodsuckers with his own body. The effect was startling. Immediately, the Sesqui-senti were thrown into complete disarray, losing their direction entirely. They wavered, bumped into each other, and many left the path completely and shambled off into the undergrowth, letting out intermittent shrill squeaks as they did, like so many directionless mice. Only when he was sure they had gone did Tarna release a gasping and perspiring Tommy.

"What on earth did you do that for?" he gasped, straightening his shirt collar and looking at Tarna as if he had been out in the sun too long.

"It was your blood they were after," he whispered. "They are drawn by the scent of human blood, as I told you."

"Then why didn't they continue?" Tommy asked, scratching his head. "*You* were in line as well."

Tarna's answer was slow and deliberate.

"I am not of human flesh," he said. "My blood is alien to them, and so it does not register with their senses. You must excuse my rather hasty action, but by behaving as I did, I effectively put a barrier between you and them, cutting off their homing in frequency. The Senti, once diverted from their chosen path, have neither the intelligence nor wit to realise their prey must be somewhere near, and wander off aimlessly and without direction. I expect Seth will not be long in bringing them back to his fold, so we must hurry. My village is but a short way off. We will be safe there, at least for the time being."

Jimmy scratched his head and, after he had shouted a few

hellos hopefully to attract attention, he decided to walk a little towards the shady wood about half a mile away. The cover looked inviting and he was ready for a rest from this beating sun. He found time to examine his surroundings more as he walked. Thick tussocky heath grass seemed to be everywhere, making him feel as if he was walking on a never-ending soft, springy mattress. Stunted bushes punctuated the landscape here and there, but the main shrub seemed to be a type of gorse in full yellow flower.

No sooner did he seem to have started towards the forest than it was upon him, its outer eves above his head, cutting out the rays of the sun. This afforded no protection, however, but seemed to change the heat from intense and direct to diffuse overall humidity, making his head swim and him feel drowsy.

"Must ... have ... sit ... down," he muttered to himself, licking his lips to try to stop them fusing together. He finally lost control of his will as the heaviness took over the driving forces of his mind. The forest seemed to be murmuring to him of cool shady copses with inviting, chuckling and trickling streams, offering rest and refreshment to his weary travel-stained limbs. On and on he stumbled, the forest ever around him like some great soothing blanket, taking him further from his path.

He stopped finally, the great black abyss not one pace away; one more step and he would experience the headlong fall to oblivion. The Great Gaping Ghyll had opened up before his unsteady steps, and his legs were about to move again, taking him forward to an uncertain end.

Chapter Four

Tarna's settlement, astride the River Lin at its shallows, was a wonderful if rather strange sight. The river was wide but reasonably shallow at this point and flowed around a large flat island upon which was set, amid a great profusion of trees and flowering shrubs, a mighty thatch-covered hut. Circular and low, it must have been fifty paces or more in diameter, with small round windows set at intervals in its smooth, matt-grey walls. Although large, from a distance the building merged in with the surroundings and became totally lost to view. The other buildings were of like construction but much smaller, and although they were many, they fitted into their undulating surroundings like so many of the hillocks around them. Apart from that, on the island there was very little vegetation, or ordered cultivation of the land, leaving the observer wondering how they obtained their food, roofing, and kindling for fire.

As they entered the outer circle of huts, Tommy experienced a strange feeling; one he couldn't readily describe or account for. It was similar to that tingling sensation he had always felt when approaching Uncle Reuben's, but somehow this time it was different. He had never been to this settlement before, even though he had visited Omni many times, or at least he didn't *think* he had.

Although, from the size of the settlement, there must have been many people living there, it seemed almost deserted. There was an oddly quiet and still feel to the place.

"Tarna," Tommy said to his companion, who was a few paces in front, "why, if your enemies are about, are there no sentries or guards, or even people about? No walls, fences or gates to keep them out?"

Tarna dropped back level with him, and tried to explain in that slow, deliberate way of his.

"The Senti do not come here," he said. "We do not need guards, for we have our Guardian who watches over us, and whose power is so strong in the surrounding area that no enemy, save Seth himself, could ever enter our stronghold. I will take you across now to be presented. Come with me."

"But how do we get across without ..?" Tommy started.

"getting wet?" Tarna finished. "Come, I will show you."

Leaving Tommy with mouth agape, Tarna leaped onto the surface of the rapids and lightly and swiftly sped across to the other side. Turning with a smile on his face, he beckoned to Tommy to join him, whose face conveyed the horror he felt at having to do this duck's dance. Tarna returned to Tommy's aid but more slowly, pointing to his feet as he did so. It wasn't until the Omnian almost reached his starting point that Tommy noticed a long row of broad, flat stones set in the riverbed with their uniformly wide tops just below the level of the river surface. Nonetheless, he still didn't feel over-safe stepping out into the unknown even with Tarna directly before him, and so his progress could only have been described as deliberate. Never before had the feel of firm soil under his feet been as welcome as when he finally came to earth not ten paces from the great hut.

His relief soon changed to wonder and amazement as the companions approached the eastern entrance, for not only was the wall smooth, it was hard as rock, and cold; a coldness which all but froze the flesh to the bone. They passed through the doorway and an eerie blackness fell about them, blocking out both sight and sound. Looking back the few paces he had come, Tommy could see no exit even though no door had shut.

"Do not be afraid," Tarna reassured. "Nought but evil needs have fear in here. Now, please close your eyes and do not re-open until I tell you."

At this command, there was no question of disobedience; the eyes simply closed without will or consent of the owner. They were opened just as abruptly soon after, to be almost drowned in a sea of intense white light, rendering him totally unseeing and helpless. The light gradually faded to a more acceptable level, allowing Tommy time to readjust his eye muscles, when to one end of the hut he caught the faint shadow of another man whose form became more and more distinct. Medium height, with a shock of curly brown hair and dancing eye brows, it was like...

"Uncle Reub...?" blurted out Tommy, and stopped in mid-word.

"What was that you said?" Tarna asked, turning to face Tommy. "I do not know what you are saying. What is 'Unclereub'?"

Tommy tried to answer but the eyes kept him motionless, and as he was released from their hold he could have sworn he beheld a twinkle of recognition. This, however, was not reflected in the man's facial expression, which remained cool and stern throughout.

"I am the Chieftain of All Omni," he boomed in a voice which fell like thunder, rupturing the profound, comfortable silence forever as it rolled around the room, reverberating from roof to wall as it went. Suddenly, when he thought it would ring in his mind forever, it stopped, leaving behind it a silence to fill the space it had created; a silence so profound it threatened to swallow him up. The silence remained, externally, but with it came long fingers probing the depths of his mind, asking, searching until every thought he had ever had was known to him. His release from this mind questioning was swift, without warning, and so sudden that Tommy was sent reeling backwards, to be stopped from falling to the floor by an enormous rush-covered couch.

"I know everything now," said the Chieftain. "Your search is almost too late. I see a hole; a black, gaping hole on the brink of which I see a shape; a small shape with coat fastened about its waist, and ..."

"Jimmy!" gasped Tommy. "That's our Jimmy! Where is he? Please tell me. I'll catch it from mum if he tears his coat or gets hurt."

"Great Gaping Ghyll," the Chieftain continued, almost ignoring Tommy's pleas. "We will bring it here."

"How on earth can you ... bring ... a ...?" he asked, slowing to a halt before he had had time to finish.

"Do not ask; simply observe and hope that the child is where he should be," replied the Chieftain.

The light both inside and out faded as they looked towards the doorway. At first nothing happened, but then, almost imperceptibly gathering in speed and clarity, a picture of the countryside, ever changing, grew out of the blackness. Tommy's mouth sagged and his head began to swim, when suddenly it stopped, as if a television picture had been frozen in mid-frame.

What he saw made him gulp and catch his breath. Small and against a great black cavernous expanse, could be seen an indistinct figure with coat fastened about his waist, socks around his ankles, and scratching his head. The telecast turned back to normal speed, with the figure not seeming to know what it was doing or where it was. One more step would mean instant death as he teetered on the brink, hesitating, undecided.

Suddenly, something seemed to click in his brain which set his feet finally in motion, and at the same time as his right foot trod air, two desperate arms grabbed him around the middle, yanking him back to safety.

The two bodies, still writhing in the grass from their exertion, finally became still, gasping heavily on top of one another. The little one turned over eventually, blinking as if he had just opened his eyes onto a brilliant day.

"Hello Tommy," it said. "What are *you* doing here?"

It was Jimmy.

"You nearly went down that great hole ... over ... there!" he blurted out, but slowed to a halt as his eyes followed his finger's indicating line. They both stared. Jimmy blinked and scratched his head again.

"What hole?" he asked, looking completely around, rather puzzled.

"Well, there *was* a hole, I promise," Tommy replied rather lamely trying to explain the hole, which no longer existed. "It must have ... Well, look, come back to the Chieftain and Tarna. *They'll* tell you there *was* a hole."

They both turned smartly around to return to the hut across the rapids to find directly before them a river and a bridge across it, but no hut. What they did see made them gasp with surprise, and their jaws sag in disbelief.

Rising out of the middle of a small lake, which formed a perfect, circular moat around it, was the most magnificent castle they had ever seen. Actually, as they had never ever *seen* a castle before, it just *had* to be the best. Large turrets with slated spires, which were decorated with flags, pennants, ribbons in a stunning array of colours, grew everywhere out of light blue, thick stone walls. One long drawbridge lay across the stretch of water, like an immense wooden rug smoothed out by giant hands.

"Just look at that...!" Tommy began but didn't finish. Several things happened at the same time, stopping them in mid-thought. A broad, hairy hand clapped itself across Tommy's face, cutting off all sound and blocking out the light, whilst at the same time an arm pinned his hands to his sides. He struggled but to no avail. He had been as effectively immobilised as if his body had been fastened in a vice. The only sound he heard, if sound is what it could be called, was a slight squeak from Jimmy, making him realise that the same fate had befallen his brother.

Heavy, grey and black clouds began to gather

threateningly to the north, as an eerie quiet settled on the land. The surrounding air gradually took on a coffee hue, subduing every other colour at will, as large icy globes of rain began to fall from the monstrous shapes created by the swirling fume above. Lightening flicked and flashed, dancing from cloud to cloud as it toyed with the other elements in its ceaseless quest to find earth.

In the light of the intermittent flashes could briefly be seen, what appeared to be, a building growing ... slowly ... out ... of ... the ... ground! Turret upon turret, stone upon stone, immeasurably strong and black - a castle; *the* castle of despair! Seth had set his foot to earth again, and his fortress had once more come to rest.

As the last stone fell into place, a great rolling boom echoed around the land, jumping from tree to mountaintop, dancing along the very cloud-face itself.

Chapter Five

"And who do you think you are," came a thin squeaky voice from somewhere in the darkness, "walking across my domain without so much as a by-your-leave?"

Although Jimmy couldn't see anything yet as all the lights had been switched off, he had a feeling that the voice was familiar. Now, where had he heard it before?

Suddenly, as if someone must have remembered you can't see very well without light, the brothers' eyes were blinded for an instant by a bath of intense white brilliance. They soon became accustomed to the brightness, as everything swam into focus. They were in an enormous room with decorated vaulted ceilings so far above them they were almost lost to sight. The walls were hung with rich-looking tapestries in golds and shades of brown and green, which spread partly onto the polished floor.

Burly guardsmen bedecked in a strange uniform they didn't recognise, surrounded them as they stood before a great oaken dais upon which sat a mahogany throne in all its glory. It was not the seat which took their gaze, but its occupant. For, sitting - or perhaps squatting might have been nearer the point - on its velvet cushion, and with an enormous ermine cloak around its back and a jewelled coronet on its head, was the most enormous green, warty toad they had ever seen. The face on top of that vast, bloated green balloon was vaguely human, and very familiar to both boys. Jimmy suddenly realised who it reminded him of, and before brother Tommy, who had had the same thought, was able to restrain him, he blurted out...

Oompah

"It's Grumblin' Gr...!"

"What's that?" came the thin reedy squeak (or was it a croak?). "What did you say?"

"Er, er, nothing," Tommy butted in, giving Jimmy a dig in the ribs to remind him to keep his mouth shut. "We, er, beg your worship's pardon, but we are, unfortunately, lost."

"Well, well," the toad replied, "and why, may I ask, are you here? Where do you come from, and why didn't you ask our permission to be here in the first place."

"Well, you see, your honour," Tommy went on again, assuming the role of spokesman, "we came to, er, visit some friends down in the settlement and ..."

"Where have you *come from?*" the voice insisted this time, as the toad turned a darker shade of green around the neck (what there was of it).

"Well, er, you see your majesty, we ..." Tommy stammered not wanting to tell the truth but at the same time not able to see a way around it.

At that precise moment, a messenger tumbled rather noisily into the chamber, obviously agitated and on some matter of urgency.

"Majesty," he burst out, after bowing three times in their custom - once to the left, once to the right, and finally to the king.

"Speak," croaked the toad.

"Majesty, the Sesqui-senti are abroad again," went on the messenger.

"That's no news," the toad croaked again. "Raise the

47

drawbridge, and ..."

"But majesty," the messenger dared to interrupt, "they are *different* this time; stronger and ... and they have no fear of water. They are crossing the outer moat, and will soon be on the island. They are changed; more powerful, evil, and ..." He trailed off to a whisper, "... our defences cannot withstand them."

"Oh dear, dear," the toad muttered, rubbing its elongated mouth with an equally long, green fore limb. "I was afraid of that. I must come at once ... supervise ... needed."

Having shot from the throne like a spring pop gun going off, he loped down the hallway, punctuating his words as he went with enormous bounds from those long, green knots of muscle and sinew he called legs. He was out of the hall in a twinkling, leaving one exhausted messenger struggling to keep pace. As he passed the startled door guards he flung back his last order.

"Captain of the Guard," he shouted, "take ... the ... prisoners ... to ... the guardroom ... I'll deal ... with them ... later "

The Captain of the Guard turned out to be the enormous body which had been gripping both their arms as they stood before the king.

"Well then, now, my lads," came a deep rumble, "you heard what his majesty said. Come along."

The two boys turned simultaneously towards the towering guard to see an enormous grin slowly spread across his face, under that huge shiny helmet.

"PC..." Jimmy started but clapped his own warning

hand across his mouth before he had had time to say any more. The grin continued to grow until it threatened to swallow the whole of his lower face. Added to this, a distinct twinkle bounced from eye to eye; a twinkle it seemed to Jimmy, which recognised what he had begun to say.

"This way then," went on the guard. "We'll have to wait down here until ..."

"Attention, Captain Mortifer!" a voice cut in as they wound their way downwards along a twisting corridor. That voice stopped the guard in his tracks and jerked his whole body to stiff attention, and for the first time in an age the brothers were released and able to walk normally. But walk they didn't, for the voice had the same effect, or nearly the same effect, on the boys. It was quiet but authoritative and firm, and as they all stood awaiting instruction, the slight figure of a young boy of about eleven stepped out from behind an enormous oaken chest.

"Highness!" Mortifer said, clicking his heels in salute, and stiffening even more rigidly to attention.

"I will take personal responsibility for the prisoners," the boy ordered. "You may go about your business."

"Highness!" the guard answered, saluting once again, turning sharply on his highly polished shoes, and stepping off down a smaller passageway to the left.

During this time the brothers had neither moved nor spoken, but Tommy, with the disappearance of the guard, had found his usual self and began to speak.

"Who are ...?" he began.

"Please have the goodness to come this way," the boy interrupted.

"I was going to say 'Who are you and where are we?'

49

but you rudely interrupted me," Tommy answered with a snort. If there was one thing he couldn't tolerate, it was rudeness.

"I beg your ..." the boy started with mouth agape, but when he saw the earnest look of annoyance on Tommy's face, mirrored in the smaller one of his brother, he changed his mind.

"I'm most terribly sorry," he went on instead. "It was very rude of me not to introduce myself."

The brothers chorused a 'Don't mention it' and waved him to continue.

"My name is Dominic," the boy went on, "and this is the castle of Oompah, King of the Western Lands of Omni."

"And ... and ..." giggled Jimmy, "was that ... that *toad* the *King*?"

"Yes, it was," Dominic answered, taking his turn now to be somewhat affronted by Jimmy's rudeness. "Yes, that is my father."

That unexpected piece of news stunned the brothers into silence, and covered Jimmy in embarrassment. He thrust his hands deep into his pockets and stared at his shuffling feet whilst muttering an uncomfortable apology.

"Don't mention it," Dominic replied. "You weren't to know. Forget it, and let's shake on it."

They all shook hands and sat down on a nearby bench to talk.

"He wasn't always like that," the prince said slowly, "like a toad, I mean."

"I was beginning to wonder how you managed to have a ... I mean, how a ..." Jimmy stammered.

"Toad came to have a human son?" Dominic finished

off his question. "He was human form originally, but that wicked magician Seth changed him into what he is because father wouldn't consent to Seth having my elder sister, Olwyn, as his wife. And so a toad he must remain until ... well, I don't know when."

"Coo," was all that Jimmy could say. All this talk of magicians, magic spells and wicked people had quite taken away his breath. Tommy was also at a bit of a loss, but he was older and had been here before, so he was the first to speak.

"Where do we go from here then?" he asked. "I don't know the way out from hereabouts. Tarna never brought me around this ..."

"Tarna?" Dominic asked a little puzzled. "Do you know Tarna?"

"Why, yes, we ..." Tommy began again but was cut short by the prince.

"Well, indeed," he went on, "you *are* welcome! Tarna, you see, is not only a great friend of mine, he is my brother."

"But, but ..." stammered Tommy, "how can he be your brother when ... you're a prince and live in a palace like this. He's only a peasant boy and lives in the Settlement over by the river. Surely ..."

"He *chose* to live there," Dominic answered quite plainly. "Didn't like the life here; always been the wild member of my family. He's been a constant source of disappointment to father."

There was silence for a short time as Dominic seemed to have fallen into deep thought. Suddenly, he jerked himself out of his reverie as Jimmy began to shuffle around in an effort to stop his empty stomach from rumbling.

"You must accept my humblest apologies for my lack of manners," Dominic said again. "My own problems have made me cast aside my first duties to my visitors and guests. You must be in great need of rest and refreshment after your trials today. Would a picnic of bread, honey, cheese and the best of last seasons crop of apples be of any use to you?"

Their chorused "Yes please!" and "Thank you very much" gave Dominic the answer he needed to lead them off to the kitchens to collect a large basket to take out to one of the inner garden areas.

As they emerged from the relative dimness of the castle into the sheltered garden, Tommy and Jimmy were dazzled by the brilliance of the afternoon sun, which was unaffected by the darkness it had witnessed earlier. The evocatively beautiful song of the lark in the upper airs carried their minds back to the fields and woods in spring and summer around their own home, and they, for the first time, felt lonely, frightened, and began to wish they were back.

The manicured and sculptured lawns could be the ideal pages for a book upon which the poetry of jasmine, veronica, weigela and lavender was written, all set out in the perfect splendour and isolation of their individual island beds and borders. There were three rustic bench seats perfectly placed to take the occasional picnic. The one they were aiming for was sheltered by an aromatic bower of arching yew which was threaded through and held together by dozens of crimson rambling roses.

"This is our private garden," Dominic broke the silence as they set to the inviting fare in the basket. "I come here often to think and just to be alone. It is a place I used to share occasionally with Tarna."

Jimmy's puzzled look prompted Tommy to describe Dominic's brother to him, and to run over a few of the adventures they had shared the last time he was in Omni.

"We became almost like brothers," Tommy explained to Jimmy. "But our meeting, the first time I came to this place, was very different from your experience so far. He seemed to be waiting for me, as if he was expecting me to be there."

Tommy continued his tales about his great friend Tarna with such enthusiasm and feeling that Jimmy felt he had known him all his life. He was sure he would know him if they were ever to meet. Dominic's feelings were mixed, however. Tarna had never shared with him the sorts of adventures Tommy described. This allowed a mixture of wonder and envy to become intertwined within him.

Silence again descended to be punctured only by the crunching of teeth against apple. In fact, the silence had grown to be so complete that even the thousands of dancing and fiddling midges had been stilled, and every sound from the three companions dropped through the air, ringing as they fell. At that moment, Jimmy realised that, although his brother was speaking, he could hear nothing of what he was saying. It was as if a deadening blanket was cutting off all sound, stifling their voices before words were issued from their lips.

At the same time, Jimmy and Tommy were gripped by

a feeling of sudden nausea so violent that they had neither choice nor control of the sickness, which surged from their bodies. Their heads began to swim alarmingly, making them unable to stand, whilst cold, clammy hands fastened themselves over their mouths and around their bodies, binding them as tightly as any stout rope. Before total unconsciousness overtook them, Tommy glimpsed a sea of the same bodies who had terrified him before.

The Sesqui-senti were abroad, and they were taken prisoner.

Their unconsciousness lasted but a short while - a brief respite of blessed relief from the nausea they had experienced before. The Senti jostled, prodded and poked their minds and bodies once more to wakeful reality, which was far worse than the dreams they might have had on the blackest of nights. Their journey, always on foot, was an unpleasant if uneventful one, covered in the main in silence, except for the crackling rattle of the Sentis' shambling gait and the pad of their shoeless feet on the soft turf.

Dusk had fallen prematurely, reducing all around to a whispering world of half-light and uncertainty. To the north the opposing cloud battalions of two warring heavenly armies vied with each other in glowering combat, each throwing towering forks of lightening, West against East. Like two great powers, mind against mind, they strove to prove their mastery, but neither gained the upper hand; each retreating to rejoin battle at some later time.

Suddenly, it was before them!

In the gloaming, the harsh, sharp outline of the seat of despair, last bastion of a world of doom and fear, appeared out of the gloom. Instinctively, Jimmy clutched at the parcel he still had under his coat. As they approached the last steps to an uncertain end, feeling it would be important, he thrust it from him into the split trunk of a gnarled and knotty oak which stood sentinel on the borders of an ancient wooded area below where the castle had come to rest.

He was only just in time. The immeasurably thick steel gates of Seth's Castle clanged shut behind them, sealing them off from the outside world.

With that last desperate clang, their world closed in on them, changing from one of sunlight and breezes to a half world of shadows, darkness and silence. It was a darkness so complete, the eyes began to feel as if they had *never* witnessed the blessed sun or those millions of winking dots at night. And silence; a deep, thick, brooding silence which wrapped itself around them. With it came the smells, which tantalised and tempted them with their favourite treats beyond imagination. Promises of whatever they wished for were laid before their eager minds. But whenever they were about to become reality, as soon as their aching mouths and stomachs were about to taste those inviting morsels, their teeth sank into empty air. As they hadn't eaten properly for quite a long time, their disappointment at missing out on what promised to be a delicious meal was understandable.

The silence didn't reign for long. Quietly at first, but increasing in intensity and volume, a voice took shape in their heads, growing in their minds until it was all they could hear.

"Welcome to my realm," it said quietly with that deceptively honeyed tongue of an insincere host. "You are guests in a place from where there is no return and in which all exits are entrances."

"But, how can we be guests if ...?" blurted out Jimmy in reply, he was rewarded by having an enormous invisible hand flapped across his mouth making it rather difficult to hold a conversation. What he *had* been going to ask was how could they be *guests* and *welcome* when they couldn't come or go as they pleased, but the chance had passed as quickly as all thoughts of food had evaporated.

The voice stopped, to be replaced by insistent, probing, searching fingers in their minds seeking out all information about their origin, their reasons for being there. Then, inadvertently, it was out! The parcel! The hint of the existence of such an object directed the questioner's full attention onto Jimmy.

"What was this 'parcel'? What was it for?"

Answers were gradually coaxed from the little boy as he felt his inner-will crumble before such a sustained onslaught.

"Where is this 'parcel' now?" the Questioner insisted. "It must be found! It has to be found for the greater good of all!"

Its whereabouts were almost revealed, when Jimmy felt a surge of power wax inside his small being, before which the Questioner faltered and hesitated, unsure of this new determined obstacle. The question was put again, more forcefully this time, but the resistance was equal to it. For an instant the full power of its fury was turned against this ... this microscopic ... thing which had had the insolence to resist the Questioner of the Glorious Lord of Seth.

Jimmy, although reinforced and supported mentally by some force outside of his understanding, was no match for such a great magician's wrath and was knocked to the floor by the intensity of his attack.

As quickly as it had appeared, the Power changed direction and was gone, giving its attention to some other field, leaving Jimmy dazed and exhausted from its suddenness. Slowly, painfully, he dragged himself to a sitting position, rubbing his head, and, for the first time since they had entered that cursed place, they could see. This world was set in a dim mistiness, which made the eyes tired and seeing very difficult, and was populated by shadows and flitting, indistinct shapes.

"You all right, Jim?" Tommy asked in a hoarse whisper.

"I ... I think so," Jimmy replied, vainly rubbing his eyes with his knuckles in an attempt to clear the fog from his head. "I'm ever so tired - and hungry. I wish we were back home with some of those bangers and bacon Mum always cooks on ... what day is it, Tom?"

"Dunno," Tommy replied, scratching his head, "but my stomach tells me it's ages since we last ate. I'm starved."

It all became clear - startlingly, painfully, desperately clear - as the mistiness vanished, leaving the brothers shocked and frightened.

Four walls, each of un-guessable thick black stone, had sprung at them from out of uncertainty, and, topped by a ceiling somewhere above their heads, they completed a dark room which proved to be their prison. A single window, three metres or so from the ground, allowed watery rays from some alien sun to bring a tiny glimmer of hope through the thick mesh covering the opening. All hope, however, was squashed when their gaze lighted on the door, which seemed to be an extension of the walls. Black, sombre, encrusted with years of damp and dirt, its only decorations were enormous, rusted iron studs and a tiny grille opening near to its top.

Too frightened to cry, Jimmy edged closer to his brother who, as old as he was, was glad of the feeling of security the closeness of his brother provided.

"Tommy?" Jimmy asked, his voice falling from his mouth with a curiously deadened sound. "Will we *ever* get out? You see, Mum doesn't know about Isaac, my gerbil, yet, and before long he'll need feeding, and besides ..." His voice faltered even though he was bravely trying to sound unworried, "... *I'm* hungry."

"Well, I..." Tommy started, but was drowned by the grating clunk of several bolts on the outside of the door being slid open. The ensuing creak of protesting hinges fixed their unblinking eyes on the gradually increasing outline of light around the doorframe. Not knowing what to expect, they were frozen as the door slowly opened; like the jaws of some preying beast.

Chapter Six

"Oh my head, my head!" Dominic groaned as he cradled his face in his cupped hands, still sitting on the floor.

The darkness in the garden had cleared almost, leaving one or two pockets of grey mist still stubbornly refusing to disperse. The sun's rays finally, after a long battle, had managed to thrust their way through the murk to re-warm and reawaken the land.

"Fear not, Dominic," a familiar voice cut through the uncanny silence. "The danger is past."

The young boy's head jerked up, a look of surprise dancing in his eyes.

"Tarna!" he finally blurted out. "How did you get here? You were out in the Settlement last I heard of you."

"The Chieftain saw troubles coming from afar. We came through as quickly as we could," Tarna answered briefly. "You we were able to save, but we came too late for the Otherworldlings. The Senti have them in their foul clutches, and by now they'll be in Seth's 'gentle' care. Their prisoners and their purpose were obviously known to them for they were taken with the least fuss. You they didn't want, but you would have lost your head had we not cut through them in time."

Dominic, forgetting his troubles and pain and glad to be able still to feel the luxury of a headache, gave out an involuntary shudder of horror and revulsion as his brother led him inside.

"But what about the Brothers?" Dominic asked as soon as they were settled in to his quarters. "Is there nothing we can do?"

"Nothing," was the quiet but definite answer from the older boy. "Once in Seth's hands, there is *no* escape. They are, I'm afraid, on their own. Any help they get must come from within, and Seth's power is ... well, look what happened to Father." His voice tailed off, leaving a deep silence in the room, which was usually bright and airy and full of the smells and sounds of nature filtering in from the garden close by.

The effects of a Seth presence were a long time wearing away, leaving the very fabric of a place steeped in his evilness.

"There is perhaps ... no, it's not possible," Tarna continued in a half-aside, talking quietly, almost to himself, with a distant look on his face.

"Go on!" said Dominic eagerly, wanting above all to help the two brothers whose friendship he courted for a fleeting moment. "You said 'perhaps'. Is there some way...?"

"Well, yes, there may be," Tarna replied hesitantly. "It's just possible - only *just* possible mind you - that the Old Man of the Mountains might be able to help."

"But ... he's ..." Dominic stammered, eyes narrowing in disbelief and a little fearful at his brother's suggestion. The Old Man had lived only in legends - a figment to frighten small boys who wouldn't behave; a shadow which sat at the back of the mind or around behind the door in a dark room.

"Yes, I know," answered Tarna. "He's been told of

60

only in stories for hundreds of years, but there are ways of summoning the help of this spirit; yes, don't be startled, his spirit lives! If it is dealt with in the right way, it can be turned to good. It is not the evil storytellers would have us believe. We must ..."

The midday bell interrupted Tarna, summoning all in earshot to the table for the afternoon repast. Reluctant to leave but not able to resist, the brothers set off down the linking corridor to their family dining area.

Resplendent in his 'king' robes, their father squatted on a raised throne-like seat at the head of the great oval table, and, as his elder son entered, the area above his enormous globe-like eyes, where there would normally have been brows, wrinkled upwards in his one show of surprise.

"We are honoured indeed," Oompah croaked in semi-mock seriousness, "to have one so important to take meat at our humble table. Were we able to make it, our bow would be of the lowest and most respectful for the occasion." He broke off to incline his bulbous head and sweep his long thin arm across his chest in illustration of his words. Tarna's only response was a slight lowering of the chin and setting his lips into a line of restraint, for he knew his father's wit of old. If he were to allow it, he could so easily be drawn into the old verbal jousts he remembered with a wince. He had come with a need for food not for exchanges to help sharpen his father's wit nor alleviate the boredom of his short fat prison.

"We were attacked by the Senti, Father," Dominic said through a mouthful of bread and honey.

"That's impossible!" Oompah blurted out. "There is no way they could have entered the Fortress."

"Impossible it may be," Tarna said not wanting to miss his opportunity, "fact it certainly is. They were 'directed', knowing what they wanted, and so shrugged aside your defences without engaging them. They carried off their prize - the two Otherworldlings."

"If that is all they came for, and took," Oompah went on with visible relief, "then we can be thankful they found nothing more useful."

"You don't seem to understand," Tarna insisted quietly. "Those two boys could turn out to be a very costly 'useless' package. They have something of enormous value that Seth obviously desires greatly, but what that is, I cannot perceive just yet. The Chieftain has encountered a blockage; a thick impenetrable mist shrouding the whole episode which he cannot pierce. He feels that if Seth discovers that which he desires, we may as well go back to hiding in caves so swift and total will be his victory."

The table company fell silent, not wishing to heed Tarna's words but not being able to avoid them. His prophecies were too real, and too close to be comfortable, and the one thing no one there wished to have disturbed was his comfort. Such talk should be confined to fairy tale telling by the fire on a cold winter's evening when all was safe in its cocoon of make-believe.

Oompah ate slowly, deliberately, that great cavernous jaw making it very difficult to chew the smaller morsels. As he dined, his mind ran back to the times before he had this ... this abominable curse to carry around with him, to the time when he was dressed in human form. As these thoughts ran through his mind, a wave of bitterness and hate for his curser rippled through his body, taking him almost to the point of despair; despair of ever being human again.

Then a sound, clear and fresh, cut through the depression, dispelling the gloom, and breathing a welcome breeze of spring into their lives. A lark had risen, sending out its fluid tones of happiness through the world. The King's warty face changed slowly, his eyes twitching towards the sound which set even his flapping feet moving in time with its message of joy. He heaved his ungainly body out of the chair and half-hopped, half-waddled across to an open window where his eyes strained to find the bird. By this time it had become a dot, a mere speck in the white-flecked blue sky above.

"That's it then," he croaked, turning away from the outside world, a new light of determination burning in his eyes. "Something must be done. We *will* sort out this upstart; this... this... Seth. The Wizard of the Enchanted Wood must be summoned and consulted, and ..."

"But ... surely we can not summon legend to our needs!" Dominic blurted out almost disbelieving what his father was saying.

"Almost unseen and largely unknown he may be," Tarna corrected, "but legend he certainly is not. By some he is known as Morgar; by others Tara-na-bos, but to most, he is Algan the Great."

Where there had been quiet before, a deeper more stunned silence set over the gathered company. The very mention of his name brought wonder to some and dread to others.

The lights in the room slowly faded leaving the semi-darkness contrasting sharply with the outside afternoon sun. Each looked surprised and puzzled, and several turned to speak but tongue had cleft to palate in an involuntary spasm leaving all present without the power to communicate with their fellows.

Their attention was drawn towards an area of silk tapestry-hung wall behind and to the right of the royal throne, where the darkness deepened and from where emanated a power of such intensity that each was hardly able to behold it for long. Softly at first, like dark treacle oozing over them, a voice poured into their minds, but then changing in depth and character, it left them in no doubt as to who was the master and from which source it came.

"I am aware of your dilemma," it said. "Seth and I are adversaries of old, and I know his mind. Do not attempt to confront him; you would be destroyed. He is of a power born of the ancient Evil and can be matched by like power only, which is outside any of your mortal capabilities. Fear not. A way will be found. My mind is turned towards it."

They were released as quickly and totally as they had been seized moments earlier, leaving their feeble minds groping and their weak, powerless bodies gasping. The room was again light, and a keen breeze disturbed the silken tapestry by the throne. There, to everyone's utter amazement, was picked out in gold and silver, a huge capital letter 'A' where previously had been woven an ancient hunting scene.

Chapter Seven

The monster-like mouth opened to its fullest extent, its yellow breath pouring over the two terrified and trembling brothers. The creaking and groaning of its protesting hinges had been replaced by a dull scraping of metal along a gritty stone floor. Jimmy's eyes remained tight shut, anticipating the worst. Tommy, however, preferred to watch the approach of whomever was entering their room with eyes narrowed ready to turn off sight should it not meet his requirements.

Quiet descended; no sound. Even the door had stopped opening, allowing the silence to grow around them.

"Don't be afraid," said a clear ringing voice, which cut through the gloom and oppression like a razor.

Slowly, like someone awakening from a long sleep, Jimmy opened first one eye, then the other, fully expecting to find that he was either at home after all or taking part in some extraordinary dream. Wasn't that the smell of frying bacon? And surely, wasn't that voice familiar? Now, where had he heard …? What he did see surprised him.

Two figures, one that of his brother, were silhouetted against the yellow light of the dungeon's outer room. The other was that of a young girl of about Tommy's age, to whom he was talking quite excitedly.

"You need not stay here," she said with a strange lilting

tone. "My uncle is occupied elsewhere, and when he throws his mind back your way, you must not be here."

"Your uncle, you say?" Tommy asked. "Who is he?"

"Why, the Lord Seth, of course," she replied.

The two boys visibly shrank away from her, immediately deciding that talking to her must be a trap. Realising from their reactions what they must be thinking, she launched in to her explanation.

"I understand what you must be thinking," she went on, "but I am linked by blood alone, and I am as much a prisoner in many ways, in this eternally mobile fortress, as you are at the moment. Seth has not always been evil you know," she continued after a moment's pause, looking at Jimmy for the first time, "but from meagre beginnings with my father, who was great in the arts of wizardry, he desired power for its own sake, and that's when he began to turn towards evil ways.

"Long years it took him to learn his art, but he had a good teacher in father, who simply poured out his knowledge into Seth, filling him almost to overflowing with his experience. When he had taken his fill, father was discarded like an empty bottle. As his knowledge, by this time, was of little use to him, father disappeared mysteriously. Some say to eternal enslavement to the will of his brother; others, including Seth himself, say he simply wandered into the wild, half-crazed by his loss of power ..."

An ominous rattle of keys somewhere in the bowels of the dungeons heralded the return of their unwelcome keeper, warning them that they ought to fly.

"I have talked overlong I fear," the girl whispered. "Come, you must be gone. They will not think to look for you until the next feeding in about an hour, and by that time you must not be around to taste their concoctions."

She closed the door behind them as they drifted silently into the outer keep outside their prison. Jimmy covered his ears expecting the door to signal their departure, but noiselessly it swung shut, securing itself with the least resistance. Their plight was simple; how to get out of a sorcerer's stronghold even with the help of the sorcerer's niece.

The journey was short in distance but long in duration, flitting as they were from pillar to pillar and dark doorway to alcove, like three grey shapes in a land of shadows. A stubbed toe or clumsy movement were all they needed to bring down a whole army of watchers onto their backs.

Although it hadn't taken them too long, Jimmy was beginning to feel the pace a little, with his joints taking most of the hammering. Sprinting, bobbing and weaving, and the sudden diving behind some enormous wooden chest, which smelled of old attics, began to take its toll. Not looking where he was going, he cast a glance over his shoulder, when he ran into the corner of a heavy, solid oak casket, half-hidden in the gloom of a deepish alcove. The air gasped and hissed out of his body like a deflated football as he sank slowly to his knees, clutching his unfortunate midriff. Away to his right, came the urgent chatter of feet on the stone floor followed swiftly by several harsh shouting voices.

"They must be down this way," one croaked. "I heard a noise."

"Yes!" shouted another. "Follow! Follow! We have

them! We have them!"

Jimmy was about to open his mouth to shout for help when a huge hand clasped itself firmly over the lower half of his face, shutting out all possibility of any sound escaping from his lips. A strong arm lifted him from the cold floor, and whisked his helpless body behind the chest into the total darkness of a close musty sort he had never experienced before; except for ... in that old cupboard under the stairs at home! That was the place daylight hardly ever saw and fresh air never sweetened; musty, dank and old, piled high with interesting and exciting rubbish. Yes, that was the smell, but it was with a different, heart-thumping excitement he faced his present situation; the excitement and fear of the unknown.

A few minutes elapsed before he was set down, gently, the right way up, and he was about to protest through a deep gasp, when he heard a whisper in his left ear advising him not to say anything yet. It was Tommy.

With mouth tightly shut and the light still turned firmly off, someone took hold of his hand to lead him to an uncertain destination. Oh how a slice of mum's suet roll and his favourite chips would have made him feel much happier and able to face what was to come.

Their progress was swift even though the darkness was thick enough to touch, and their guide was either an expert or a night animal, so straight and unerring was his track. Sweet, cool and hot, stifling air attacked Jimmy's bare face and arms from tunnels opening to left and right, but nothing slowed their rate or deflected their course.

Suddenly he was stopped by having his nose squashed

without warning between the shoulder blades of the person in front.

"Steady on, now! I'm not a wall!" It was Tommy's voice, and oh how glad the younger brother was to be able to communicate with someone.

The light, without his really realising it, had grown gradually around him, becoming more diffuse and allowing him to see at last who his guide was.

"But … but …" he stammered in disbelief at seeing only Tommy and the young girl before him. "Where's the big … ? And how … ?"

It was obvious from the look of mild amusement in her eyes and the slight smile playing around her lips that there was more to her than he understood. He halted in mid-sentence and took to sucking his bottom lip, a puzzled frown on his brow.

"There is no need to worry," she smiled. "A sorcerer's daughter may dare and achieve almost anything. Take comfort that through there is your escape, and whatever lies in store for you both."

She swept her hand in front of them, directing their gaze towards a dancing curtain of grey mist across their exit from this den of sorcery, and their entrance to the unknown. As the first wisps of the curtain played across their feet a thought struck Tommy:

"We don't even know your name," he croaked hoarsely, looking back over his shoulder.

Instantly, almost in anticipation of the question the sweet name "Miriel" floated back to them through the mists, and as it brushed their ears, a feeling of lightness and hope surged through their bodies. The mist finally closed around them and all trace of their companion was lost. They were finally on their own, and the only way left for them was to go forward.

"Well, Jim," Tommy said after a few moments of thoughtful hesitation, "this is a rum how-do-you-do and no mistake. We can't go back; forward is completely unknown, and all in all …"

"We're lost," Jimmy interrupted.

"Correct!" Tommy answered. "Well, it's for sure we can't stay here. Time's getting on and staying here's just wasting it. So I vote we go on. What do *you* say?"

"OK by me," Jimmy answered. "I don't know what day it is even, so we've nothing to lose."

So, with a last look back and a nod to each other, the two brothers set off deeper into the mist, accompanied by a strange musical wheeze, which sounded as if the wind was trying to breathe life into a set of worn-out old bagpipes.

On they trudged, able to see nothing but a white blanket mist which enveloped them totally. It was not your usual damp, smelly, choking mist, really not a mist at all, only a mass of white, which painted out all the surroundings.

Stronger than ever through this white blanket, with other senses heightened by lack of sight, came the equally evocative evidence of an exotic countryside: scents and sounds such as they had never experienced before nor ever dreamed could exist. The sappy, resinous smell of a spring morning's pine forest mingled with the salt tang of a sou'westerly from the sea, woven around by the equally incongruous sounds of the strident, plaintive cry of a gull superimposed on the back-drop of a country meadow in early summer.

Confused and yet overjoyed at the re-awakening of some of their half-forgotten memories, Tommy and Jimmy stumbled on through undergrowth they couldn't see but felt, as its springy whip-like grass stems returned to their starting places on their passing.

"I'm thirsty," gasped Jimmy after half an hour or so, "and I …"

"Sh!" Tommy hissed, stopping sharply and grabbing his brother. "Over there," he whispered, "see, the mist is thinning out, and I can see … people!"

"Where? Where?" Jimmy asked, craning his neck and shuffling around in what felt like heath tussocks under foot. "Show me. I … Arghh! My shin! My leg!"

He had broken away from Tommy's grasp, and collapsed somewhere in the thickening mist. His pained groans and gasps came from somewhere below the knee height of his brother, who immediately dropped to a crouch to feel around for his younger brother.

"Jim. Jim," he croaked. "Where are you? Groan a bit and then I can get a fix on your position."

Jimmy didn't find that remark in the least funny, but obliged with a heart-felt moan nonetheless, which resulted in his brother finding him.

"Careful, can't you?" Jimmy complained at last. "That's my eye you've got your great … elbow … in!"

Jimmy had finally realised that the mist had disappeared, as if some huge vacuum cleaner had removed all trace of the obliterating nuisance, and what he saw in no way even approximated what he had imagined. Barren hills are what they saw, bare of all vegetation apart from the springy tussocky heath grass they had been stumbling along, and mountains - stretching endlessly in a great crescent far away into the blue haze off northwards and out of sight. They had been to the mountains for holidays many times before father had died, but compared with the grandeur and scale of these, their mountains were as a rash on an animal's back.

Jimmy's gaze swept around following the range until his eyes became watery with the strain. On their return journey, his eyes lighted on the object which had brought about the untimely meeting of his knees and the ground. Cold, it felt against his skin, and hard and unyielding under his hand.

"But ... but ..." he stammered, taken very much aback by its sudden appearance. "It's a ..."

"Grave," Tommy finished off for him. "Overgrown it may be, but still very much a ... grave ..."

His matter-of-factness quickly evaporated on looking up from the hard, glossy rectangularity of the grey granite grave surround, withstanding the continual onslaught of weed and weather, to catch the shadowy outline of some indistinct figure in his eye corners. He nudged his brother who had already seen their ghostly spectator and was slowly dragging himself to an upright position, eyes firmly fixed on the apparition. Large in the extreme, with huge hairy arms folded across its chest like scaffolding, its unblinking eyes peered out of a face totally surrounded by black, grey-flecked, dishevelled hair, fixing them to the spot as effectively as tying them with rope.

The Old Man of the Mountains sought an explanation from those disturbing his rest!

Chapter Eight

The darkening storm gathered about the pinnacles and battlements of Seth's castle. Black clouds formed their battalions, marshalling their dark troops ready for battle with the Master of Mystery. Lightening began to flicker and play, adding a silver circlet to the crown of clouds the castle already displayed.

The first rolling clap of thunder startled the surrounding countryside and even rattled the thick stone battlement tops. This would be a conflict to end all conflicts, and one in which the elements, after centuries of perseverance, would crush utterly the upstart magician who had tried - and succeeded for the most part - to tame them to his will.

The crash, although expected and prepared for, still took participant and spectator by surprise, stunning even the hardiest of animals into immediate submission. Yet the castle simply sat, amidst its bushes and trees, like the bones of the earth out of whose rocks it had gradually grown over the years.

Suddenly, when the intense blue flash of the storm had stopped printing tiny replicas on the inner black velvet backdrop of the eye, it was gone! The castle had disappeared as quickly as it had come, leaving a deeper, darker gap in the countryside.

Tommy and Jimmy felt instantly the moment the

disappearance had taken place.

"But … Tom … the par…!" was all Jimmy was allowed to say by his brother, who clapped his hand tightly across his mouth, in the meanwhile whispering to him not to disturb the guest to their homely surroundings.

The figure didn't move. Motionless, his unblinking eyes bored through their minds, searching, probing and asking. Where had they experienced that before? Yes, of course …!

"Seth!" blurted out Jimmy with the impetuosity of youth. "You're … !"

"Seth, and not Seth," came the overriding reply, but the lips did not utter those words; they were not heard but felt. Jimmy was beginning to wonder if in fact the ears were of any use at all in this land, nobody much seemed to use them; at least, not for communication anyway. That was one of the things about this country he would alter if he ever became king; that and things like better catering facilities, and more toilets. Why didn't they ever…? His mind was wrenched unceremoniously back to the attention of their visitor, who was beginning to become a little irritated by the small boy's lack of attention.

Now, that attitude seemed to strike a familiar note somewhere in Jimmy's head; a note of recognition. The face, covered as it was by so much facial undergrowth, where had he seen …? The thought suddenly struck him between the eyes, in between the probing and dark words.

"Mr Bolam!" he burst out without thinking about the consequences of such impetuous actions.

"You seem singularly intent on distracting by your inattention, young man, so I will fix your thoughts by speech," the apparition burst in rather annoyed, seeming much less like a ghost than at first suggested.

Yes, that was definitely Mr Bolam, Jimmy thought; that turn of temper, that sarcasm, that ...

His tongue suddenly stuck to the roof of his mouth, making him unable to open his lips or to focus his attention on anything other than the visitor. His eyes were drawn, reluctantly, to his form, which grew brighter as the surroundings became dimmer and more indistinct, drawing in a thick grey mist to form a halo around his shape.

"I am Gor-ifan, whom some would name The Old Man of the Mountains," he said in a voice which seemed to come from somewhere below them, struggling to take form and give substance to its user. "I am - was - brother to the Wicked Lord of Seth. I *was* the Seth before my brother, Tar-igor, banished me to a half-life in the waiting Land of Four, and took my title and my birthright, becoming himself the Seth."

There was a momentary pause as the mist threatened to overwhelm him, but he gradually reasserted his mastery and continued.

"You two, I deem, may be able to aid my cause. You will come with me."

The change was sudden, unexpected, as the mist darkened and began to move outwards, away from Gor-ifan, like a window slowly demisting. At first, the space behind him was dark and indistinct, but as the mist retreated so the light grew in intensity and colour until it reached its final pale yellow.

The land they walked in was flat, featureless and bare of all save themselves. As they watched, tiny black dots appeared on the yellow land and began to grow upwards, straight and tall, as if making up for lost time. Within a few minutes, a forest of sapling pine trees had sprouted thick and dark before their disbelieving eyes. Within the time it would take to plant one of the trees, a thick forest of black spruce had reached maturity. To the south of the forest, directly before their feet, a bright silver ribbon trickled, grew and flowed in its quest for the sea.

This land creation continued, unchecked, unabated, its virgin birth showing none of the usual growing pains. The plan had been formed long ago, awaiting a trigger; that trigger had been sprung. Nothing could now halt its progress.

As the ribbon of a river reached its destination, the brothers became aware of a darkness creeping over them. Startled, they looked around, to find they were standing under the eaves of a great, dark forest where once there had been plains. Dark, forbidding trees of a type unknown to them formed an eerily quiet body, like some still but watchful beast. For this was no haphazard collection of individual trees, the wood had a corporate life, and it breathed as a single vast being.

Again, as they watched, unable to speak or move, dark mists formed and wove themselves around the tree boles, bringing to the forest a profound feeling of mystery, and to the boys a deep sense of unease.

"Where have you brought us?" Tommy asked of Gorifan, turning to face him. His question lay where he had dropped it, unanswered. Gor-ifan was no longer there. They were again utterly alone!

As near a mixture of panic and relief swept over Tommy and Jimmy in a joint involuntary spasm, feeling fear and joy at once again being alone. But were they…?

"I'm glad *he's* gone," Jimmy finally ruptured the silence.

"Yes, but don't you get the feeling that we're being watched by … something or other, out there?" Tommy said with a grimace and a vague sweep of his arm.

"I suppose you're right," Jimmy answered. "There's something vaguely unsettling about a place that doesn't behave as it should. But then that could be said about the whole of this country. I'm beginning to wish Uncle Reub …"

"Shsh!" interrupted his brother in a low whisper. "Be quiet. I can hear something rustling over there."

The mist, which by this time had completely enveloped them, suddenly rolled away, leaving everything clear and clean and new. They were now deep in the forest with the feeling that they were standing on un-trodden earth in a place where fear had no substance or place.

Again they stopped, taken utterly by surprise, for in a small clearing, surrounded by hawthorn bushes, was a large flat stone, set on its end against a rock face about man high. Tommy turned to point this out to his brother, but he became somewhat puzzled to find it had disappeared.

"Must have been dreaming," he muttered, shrugging off his mistake.

"No; look!" Jimmy whispered, nodding towards the clearing again. This time Tommy gasped, for the stone, which must have weighed half a ton or more, had been

77

rolled back to one side, revealing a dark hole. Leading up to this hole were five smoothly cut steps inviting entry to its gloomy interior. Nothing else could be seen.

They blinked, and on opening their eyes again, they were surprised to see the clearing and cave entrance still there, but with one subtle change. A light now poured down the steps making entrance to those secrets beyond a little more inviting.

To Jimmy, the welcome was unmistakable; it said 'come in'. So he skipped across to the clearing and had set foot on the bottom step before his brother had had time to think, let alone move. As his foot touched the *top* step - the last before the threshold - Tommy suddenly came to life, finally realising his brother was about to disappear again. Mother wouldn't be at all pleased if he lost him again, so he had no alternative but to bound after him.

"Whoa, Jim!" he shouted. "Hang on a bit. Wait for me! We ought to …"

He didn't manage to finish his sentence. There sprang up a hoarse screech behind him as something whistled through the air. It stopped its flight when it met the back of Tommy's head with a dull sickening thud, pitching him forward onto his face across the flight of stone steps not five paces behind his brother. The lights went out suddenly in his brain, leaving him helpless prey to his unseen assailant.

The darkness was total. Jimmy could neither see nor hear anything. The urge to enter had been irresistible, and had seized him from across the clearing. Now he was in the cave, he was not quite as sure, but the urge was no less

78

strong. His eyes were useless to him at the moment, but to compensate, his sense of smell had been heightened, giving him scents he knew and loved – new oak and leather. A thought flicked across his mind, leaving him grasping and unsure. He *knew* where he'd experienced those same smells previously; on one occasion only. A strange sort of light began slowly to well up from the floor as if filling a transparent vessel with its golden warmth.

There was nothing he could recognise at first, but as the light grew, spread and intensified, an image began to clarify in his confused brain. Suddenly the light rang out into its final startling clarity, and Jimmy's confusion was complete. He was as a sleeper gradually surfacing through the various levels of consciousness until the ultimate emergence imprinted a picture of reality upon his mind.

That scene before him now, although experienced once only before, was part of his conscious and subconscious knowledge in such a way that it would never be forgotten. In all details save one, the scene before him was …

"…Uncle Reuben's study!" he gasped, hardly able to believe what he saw. Had he dreamed *all* his adventures, or had they been part of Reuben's own story? The great desk, the wall trappings, the shelves were those he had indelibly fixed in his mind's eye - everything was exactly as he had remembered. Then his gaze was riveted by the one detail which told him immediately that he was somewhere else… the floor was sawdust and cork chippings, and not the deep pile carpet of his uncle's study.

"You are correct … and yet not so," boomed a voice from across the room. It came from a figure that Jimmy hadn't noticed, half-hidden beside one of those panelled book shelves, and it made him start rather. He swung round on his heels to see where the voice had come from, and on locating the person, let out an involuntary gasp of shock and surprise to see ...

"Uncle Reuben!"

"I am Algan," the voice boomed again, ignoring his statement, "and you are now in my realm."

Realising too late that he had betrayed the one confidence his uncle had wanted him to guard - the existence of his study - Jimmy's chin dropped to his chest and he stared at his uneasily shuffling feet as they made symmetrical patterns in the oak chippings. Suddenly, he felt his face being lifted, but not by Algan, who had remained motionless where Jimmy had first seen him. Face level with the magician's, their eyes met and the boy's mind was held, and *then* it was that he knew his secret was safe. During that short time, Jimmy's mind was stripped of all relevant information, and his thoughts released as quickly as they had been seized.

"We will talk later," Algan burst through the barrier of silence. "As much information relevant to your needs I already have, I see no point in continuing for the present, and ..."

"Excuse me for butting in," Jimmy asked politely, but getting a little more fidgety, "can you tell me where my brother, Tommy, is? You see, he came here with me, and now I seem to have lost him."

Algan beckoned Jimmy to follow, and they set off at a reasonable speed towards the inner door, which no doubt led to somewhere interesting.

The inner part of the cave was entirely different from anything he had ever seen before. In fact, the two parts were so different that they could have been in separate worlds.

They entered now a series of corridors - borings might have been nearer the mark - which could have been caused by some giant passing worm, the sides of which were smooth to the point of glassiness. The floors were still covered by the same universal cork and sawdust, which lay so thickly on the ground that the only noise they could hear was a swish and squeak as they padded along.

There were no adornments to the circular walls except for the occasional strange-looking serpent lanterns casting an eerie soft green light everywhere. He was so entranced by the appearance of it all that he never noticed the transition from the corridor to another, similar, room. In fact, he wasn't even certain there had been a transfer; if there had, the door must have vanished for certainly no door was to be seen anywhere in that room.

He allowed his gaze to wander around the room, jumping from groups of bottles and jars on tables to globes and maps, to other pieces of equipment he didn't recognise at all. His eyes skidded to a halt as they caught sight of a long, low table covered by a white mark-free cloth; and it was there his heart lurched and his breath almost stopped, as a gasp sped from his lungs to explode from his mouth into the room.

Under that sheet lay a body, totally covered to the chin. The skin, white almost to the point of transparency, and the form were those of a boy; eyes fast shut, breathless, still, frozen in that last eternal sleep of death.

It was Tommy.

Chapter Nine

The night was black; blacker than had been seen for many an age. An occasional wandering chink in the cloud curtain allowed enough light from the intense blue moon to pour onto the rise and fall of the Southern Downs, crowned by the mysterious, ancient standing stones. Smooth, round, hard and black, the stones had been set on the uppermost rise of the range of hills many ages of man before, for what reason no one now knew, save the lore masters and magicians of that realm. Rumour and legend had it that they were part of the magic of old, and had since become a trysting place, a refuge for restless spirits and evil beings. Black they were; blacker than the surrounding gloom, picking them out like a brooding menace in the shadows.

At that moment, the cloud split, wide enough to allow the pent up blue light to cascade to the earth like a released waterfall. The light splashed across the black surface of uprights and crosspieces, gathering all to spotlight the great arch underneath, highlighting a black solitary figure on horseback below.

The Horseman! The Wandering Rider! It was him! Figure of legend, phantom of nightmare, he had come again, as in the past, at a time of greatest strife and need. Why had he come? What would be his course? Steed and man were as one, a great shadow cloaked in black. No covering to his head he wore, only a black flowing mane of hair. Motionless they stood, immobile; statues both but for the slight flicking of the horse's tail.

The last despairing trace of a dying moon splashed desperately across the Rider's head and face revealing that there was no face!

Hair encircled the featureless visage perfectly but neither eyes nor nose nor mouth looked out from this mask of doom, making it all the more terrifying and terrible to behold.

Suddenly the horse's tail stopped in mid-twitch, the horseman stiffened and half-stood in the stirrups, head slowly turning from side to side. Those acutely sensitive ears had detected something in the upper airs, something which made their whole corporate being bristle with anticipation.

There was a flash of silver spur and a breeze of mystery as the moon disappeared behind a small cloud. When the orb dared to come out of hiding, the great archway between the standing stones was once again empty. Only his presence could be detected, a much darker imprint on the skyline, which was becoming lighter by the minute as morning swiftly approached. His spirit would not again be easily stilled in that age of the world whilst strife was ever present, and often was his rumour to be heard passing as a bird in the night.

Tears streaming down his face, Jimmy shuffled across to the motionless, un-breathing body of his brother. Near the table, tentatively he stretched out his hand towards the white covering shroud, but involuntarily shrank away before touching it. His hand fell, lifeless, to his side, and his shoulders slumped in resignation, as slow, quiet sobs convulsed his small frame.

"Why are you weeping?" rumbled the magician, an arm around the heaving shoulders.

"My brother … Tommy … he's …" sobbed Jimmy, overcome at last.

"But," Algan interrupted, "there is no need; see, the nostrils. Watch."

Jimmy's eyes became riveted to the lifeless form before him. At first nothing. He could see nothing but the distortions caused by the tears filling his eyes. Slowly, almost imperceptibly, as the tears dried and left his vision clearer, he thought he detected a slight twitching around the nose … but no, it must have been a trick … No! It was no trick! There it was again! Jimmy gulped, rubbed his eyes so as not to be mistaken, and looked again, more closely this time. Movement there certainly was, making him realise that he was not mistaken. His brother was alive!

"But … but … he's ALIVE!" he shouted finally, as Tommy's eyelids flickered and slowly opened.

"Who on earth's making all that din?" a faint and trembling voice asked from the table, "and where's tea? I'm starved."

"I had the most horrid dream," muttered Tommy through a mouthful of Algan's best seed cake. The colour was now flooding back to his cheeks, which were round and firm again thanks to the magician's wonderful cuisine. "It was like being eaten alive by an enormous bird with a cruel crooked beak and a taste for human flesh." He paused and shuddered at the thought, but continued with his cake, irrepressible to the last.

"It was no bird I can assure you," Algan interrupted the intervening silence, "but something which would have turned out to be infinitely worse - capture by the Senti and interrogation by Seth himself."

"But, we've already…" Jimmy protested.

"Been captured and questioned?" Algan finished his sentence with a grim smile.

Jimmy's jaw dropped open in amazement, and his eyes widened to saucer shape. His unspoken question about how he knew remained unspoken, but had been answered from within by the Great Magician.

"He knows rather more about you than before," Algan went on, "and is now no doubt furious that he should have let you slip away so easily. Next time there will be *no* escape."

His words left the boys in no doubt about their fate should they succumb once again.

"But, the parcel!" Jimmy burst in again, remembering his loss. "I left the parcel when we were captured last time."

"That *is* bad news," Algan answered quietly, a look of concern spreading across his eyes. "Should he manage to get his hands on it, there would be no end to his mastery. Where did you leave the parcel? It must be found."

"You don't seem to understand," Jimmy said quietly and slowly. "Before we were taken into the castle, I pushed it into the cleft trunk of an old tree before the moat… "

"And we think the castle and all the surrounding area have disappeared," Tommy interrupted, wiping the food from his mouth.

A profound silence fell over the room; so deep, in fact, that they could feel it around them. It felt almost as if they had climbed *inside* Algan's *mind*, with his thoughts blotting out everything, preventing even their movements. They were like statues, frozen in a timeless void of silence, neither able to move nor even to think.

"That is serious news indeed," Algan broke the silence again, bringing them both to earth with a jolt, enough to make Jimmy's teeth rattle and Tommy's cake-filled stomach lurch. "However, I have searched the area ...", he paused enough to catch the look of utter disbelieving amazement on their faces, and then continued in explanation, " ... in my mind, and I can find three split-boled trees large enough to take a parcel. Nearer than that I cannot tell. You must return - for I could not do it for you - and retrieve that which you have lost. It is of the utmost urgency that you succeed. If you don't ..."

His voice tailed off into a hidden whisper of despair which chilled their bones.

"Algan?" Tommy asked, turning towards the old magician as they sat quietly and comfortably in the living part of the cave.

"Yes, my boy?" he said, drawing on an enormously long curved clay pipe from which he sent smoke rings of varying size and colour to delight and entertain the brothers. There was already a stack of eight hovering by Jimmy's shoulder, rather like a pile of miniature quoits ready to be thrown.

"What hit me?" he went on. "You know, just before your cave entrance."

"It was a flying Senti," the magician replied in a matter-of-fact sort of way; "and ..."

"I thought you said nobody could enter your forest without your consent," Jimmy interrupted, somewhat puzzled by all this talk of Senti in his enchanted forest.

"I could not pick him out until it was almost too late," Algan replied. "He was catapulted, and had he met you a few seconds sooner, before the failure of his trajectory, you would no longer be the owner of that fine head of yours."

Tommy gulped, and his initial reaction was to clasp his hands to his throat and neck in order to keep his head where it should be - on his shoulders.

"It was a very long chance," the magician went on, "but one which almost succeeded. As it was, the creature came out of your shadow long enough for me to perceive it was there, and to lessen its impact. The rest you know. You were very close to that eternal abyss when I brought you in; almost too far gone to rescue, I was able to call on deeper powers to help bring you back."

The room began to fade and spin, and his senses started to swing like one of those enormous clock pendulums gone mad. The last thing Tommy remembered was the hugely beaming face of Algan, filling completely his eyes and mind.

Sleep is a wonderful thing; too little of it and you don't function properly; just the right amount, and everything is just fine. Jimmy and Tommy had been suffering from too little for too long, so the sleep they experienced was especially refreshing, with that special added ingredient from the magician which was secret to him alone. Deep, and filled with the most pleasant dreams of home, mum's cooking and all those things which had occupied their every waking moment in the wild, that sleep took them through the barriers of fatigue and into a new stage of alertness. Even though they had slept for only an hour or two, it didn't seem as though they had even closed their eyes at all, but that sleep and waking were all part of the same pleasant process.

"The parcel," Algan went on when the boys were fully ready to understand what he had to say, "has to be found and returned. I think that the trees you talked about, and in particular the split one, are still there, teetering on the edge of the great gaping hole that is the legacy each Seth appearance and disappearance leaves. You will have to go alone. I shall not be able to come with you."

"But ... but ..." stammered Jimmy.

"We were kind of counting on your support," Tommy interrupted.

"I *cannot* be with you," Algan repeated, "but do not despair. One whom I trust well and whose power equals mine but in another direction, shall watch over you, and, should the need arise, render such aid as necessary."

"Who will this person be?" Tommy again insisted. "How shall we recognise him?"

"You will *know*," Algan reassured. "The time is now right. Further delay should not impede your quest. The time of the Otherworldlings, fast approaches. I say only to you, keep the Craggs of Gotts Point in your sights and do not deviate towards the Old Watch Tower. There you will not find the end to your search."

They were then aware of a keen air in their nostrils, a slight breeze through their hair, and Algan's voice in their minds only. The cave was no longer around them, but the open country lay in front and the sinister black silhouette of the Craggs lay before them in the distant gloom of approaching night. On an instinct, the boys turned sharply to catch a final glimpse of the Enchanted Forest, to find that the land between them and the Western Mountains was open, with no trees to be seen anywhere.

"Well, Jim," Tommy shrugged, "we may have dreamt it, but those Craggs are real enough. So, come on! Let's get on!"

"I'm afraid Tom," Jimmy said huddling closer to his brother as they forced a way as quickly as possible through the dense, thorny undergrowth.

"Don't worry about it," his brother replied. "So am I, but we must keep on. Everything depends on us. This darkness should help even though I can't see the way very well."

The darkness hissed as its silence deepened around them. The breeze they had experienced earlier had almost imperceptibly deserted them, leaving a close stifling atmosphere which before long had them gasping for air in the increasingly frequent rest stops they made. Bushes and trees loomed and lurched at them out of the darkness as they blundered on in their haste to be free of this tight, claustrophobic feeling. They didn't seem to have been moving very long but the magic of this place was such that they felt as if an age had passed since their encounter with Algan in his cave. How could they have travelled so far? Or was it so far? Was this Algan's doing? Was he helping them after all?

Tommy stopped dead in his tracks, and, grasping Jimmy's arm pulled him to a halt by the bole of a huge oak tree.

"What's the matter?" asked Jimmy.

"Sh! Sh!" hissed his brother, half crouching as if ready to spring away. "Listen!"

"I can't hear anything..." Jimmy whispered, the perspiration now running freely down his face and back, "...except for a slight crackling of dry leaves on the branches around ..."

"There is no wind!" Tommy replied. "Besides, all the leaves are still green ..."

"What is it then?" Jimmy asked, tiny little prickles of fear beginning to creep slowly up his spine. "It's getting closer and louder, and seems to be spreading all around us."

"I don't ... oh my god!" Tommy uttered, dropping to an almost inaudible croak. "Over there...look!"

Through the gloom, some fifty or so paces away, a faintly luminous grey mass oozed between the trees and shrubs towards them. The crackle and rattle of member against member was unmistakable, and as the mass moved nearer, dozens of individual grey bodies could be picked out with ease. The leading one sent out a high, shrill squeak that homed the others onto their prey. The Senti would not fail this time.

The boys, eyes wide with utter terror, finally tore themselves away from the spot to which they had been rooted, mesmerised, and turned to flee. They were again stopped in their tracks, as hoards of Senti seemed to grow out of their surroundings to cut off their retreat. They were trapped! Those sightless faces, eager for a capture to return to their master, swarmed over the intervening swathes of land with unerring accuracy towards their goal.

Chapter Ten

The room was dim, and the occupants indistinct in the gloom. A thick, musty, damp smell hung in the still atmosphere inside, making it difficult for all, but those used to it, to breathe without gasping. Streamers of watery light crawled through several small cracks in the reed walls, casting an eerie light across the room.

An overwhelming silence gripped everyone there, trying to choke the mind as the atmosphere tried to choke the body. The only sound to be heard was the heavy grunting and moaning of someone engaged in intense physical combat, although no other movement could be seen.

Gradually the eyes accustomed themselves to the gloom, and as they fought their way around this enormous enclosure, they were finally drawn to a dark, bearded, solitary figure in an enormous heavily-cushioned wicker chair which was set on a small platform. The occupant of the chair sat perfectly still but in a strange way that looked most uncomfortable. Hands on knees, shoulders bent slightly forwards and very straight, his eyes were tight shut. More and more frequently his silhouette, his whole outline, was lit by some deep power.

A flash! The hair and face became wreathed in intense

blue light, giving a profoundly sinister look to the strange being, and at the same time, his breath shortened and began to escape in great gasps.

The suddenness of the ensuing explosions and flashes of lightening took everyone off guard, except for the central figure. The light disappeared totally, to be replaced immediately by dancing, red lines of electric power which wove and jerked around him.

Silence once again enveloped them, to be broken only by the central figure, the Chieftain of All Omni. With a cackle which grew into a low rumbling laugh, he flung his arms wide, and as he did so, light slowly began to stream into the room from every conceivable angle, filling all space like a great glass bowl with pure, white light.

"I have you now, my friend," the Chieftain muttered to the air. His mental struggle with the Lord of Sorcery was over and he had proved to be the Master. The Chieftain's hour was fast approaching, and Seth's trough of despair would follow in its wake. Seth had finally met his match!

Boom! Boom! The distant roll of thunderous drums mingled terrifyingly with the screech of the Sesqui-senti as they swamped the land around the boys with the presence of their master. Taking courage and survival in both hands, the brothers flattened the leading bunch with half-branches torn from sapling trees. Bolstered by their success with the first few, they stood back-to-back bracing themselves for the next onslaught. When they saw the extent of the mass of Senti, they began to despair.

"We can never beat off that lot!" yelled Jimmy, arms aching already with the exertion.

"Come on!" Tommy signalled. "Up into this tree. The branches are low enough."

Tommy heaved his brother into the lower branches and twigs whilst kicking over one of the attacking creatures that came too close. Jimmy scrambled further into the safety of the dense foliage, but Tommy was just a little too long in swinging up. As Jimmy looked down, he was horrified to see his brother washed over by a great wave of white bodies and dragged down by the sheer size of numbers.

"Get back! Get on up before …" Tommy yelled, but was cut off in mid-sentence.

It was a terrible dilemma Jimmy found himself in. If he went back to help, what use could he be against so many? Yet, how could he leave his brother without trying to help? At least, they would be captured together.

As he turned to descend, to take up the Last Battle, he was startled again to hear the rattle of side drums, accompanied this time by the blare of brazen trumpets. The sight beneath him almost made him fall from his perch. Men in green had sprouted from nowhere, and were striding through the masses of Senti, swords and axes swinging, like farmers through a field of corn. Heads rolled and bodies were tossed aside like handfuls of chaff in the wind.

Apart from the swish of blades, the roll of drums, and the squeals of the Senti, the whole operation was carried out with silent efficiency.

Tommy was soon relieved of his burdensome overcoat of white bodies, and was brought to a standing position by two enormous, silent guardsmen. Grim-faced and tight-lipped, they set him on his feet between them, a position soon also to be assumed by his brother, and there they remained until the last Senti had been crushed back into the earth.

"What are *you* then?" one of the guards growled when all the Senti had been removed, a frown threatening to send his already overgrown eyebrows thundering into the rest of his face.

"Can't look up at his face for long," Jimmy began thinking. "He's too high and I would get neck ache."

"You will have to come with us," growled the mountainous guard. "Our chief will want to see you."

The guardsmen spent the next few minutes jabbering at each other in some language which was utterly unintelligible to the boys, so they stopped listening and trying to make out what they were saying. Eventually, when the conversation had receded, Tommy and Jimmy were picked up, tucked each under an enormous hairy armpit where they stayed quite comfortable, en route to the "chieftain" of this particular tribe, whoever he was. They didn't have to wait too long.

Long before they saw him, they felt his presence; stifling and powerful, it made their heads spin and ears pop.

"I'm going to get a head …" Jimmy started.

"Silence!" growled one of their guardians. "You will not speak unless told to do so."

Jimmy reddened slightly around the cheeks, which showed he was growing up considerably and learning to accept orders without question; without becoming acutely embarrassed and wanting to hide behind mum. The length of time they had spent in the wild certainly had done *something* for him. *What* he was not at all sure.

He turned slowly to look at his brother and was puzzled to see his mouth open, and a look of blank amazement on his face. He turned himself to follow the same direction as Tommy's gaze. What he saw, he didn't understand, but it filled him with wonder and fear all the same.

Away to his right, on the edge of the clearing they now found themselves in, there was an indistinct mass of grey mist, constantly moving and changing shape. Basically it was the size and shape of a man, but the mist was so effective a screen, neither features nor details could be seen. After a few moments watching, the observer was left with the feeling that there was in fact nothing there at all; had it not been for the power! Whilst its intensity waxed, the observer could do nothing of his own free will. The Thing was in complete control.

Suddenly, their minds were seized, searched thoroughly for a few moments, and then released. As that snap of

96

release happened, their eyes cleared, and the mist had gone. In its place stood a man, the like of which they had seen before only in fantasy story books. A little shorter than their guardians his personal stature and magnetism were much greater. His long flowing white hair and beard cascaded over a powerful and youthful frame, and were circled about the forehead and temples by a small silver band. No other mark of clothing distinguished him from the others, save a belt of leaves around his green tunic.

"I am Por, Chief of the Wandering People," his deep voice rumbled over them. "We do not welcome strangers, but your case I will hear. Come."

As they turned to move away from the scene of destruction, out of the corner of his eye, Tommy caught a glimpse of something by a clump of beech saplings. Something dark, sinister and terrible - a black horse and rider, he thought, but he could see no detail. He turned to summon his brother, but when he returned his gaze, he could see only a deeper shade in the gloom around.

"I could have sworn…" he half-said to himself, not meaning to be heard.

"What did you say?" asked Por, turning sharply.

"Nothing, really," answered Tommy, scratching his head, puzzled. "I thought I saw a black horseman, over there by those trees, but …"

Por's face was impassive, showing no sign of emotion. "As you see," he continued after a few moments' silence, "there is no-one. You *imagined* you saw something."

"Well," Tommy muttered quietly, "we had rather thought you could sort of give us some direction…"

"To what end?" Por interrupted at last, wishing to cut short the unnecessary intrusion of useless conversation.

"To find our parcel, of course!" Jimmy continued, quite put out by this great chieftain's abrupt and rather direct manner.

"You have not told me the importance of this *parcel*," Por went on becoming more insistent, fixing Jimmy with a piercing glare, which made him want to shrivel up inside, "and why you need to recover it."

Jimmy shifted and shuffled uneasily, casting a nervous glance across at his brother who was feeling equally uncomfortable under this sharp, pointed questioning.

"Well, er..." he squeaked almost inaudibly, when suddenly, shutting his eyes, he launched into the whole story, like a flood being released from behind a floodgate. To Jimmy it seemed to last an eternity, but in fact was only a few minutes.

He stopped as suddenly as he had begun, waited a few seconds, and then tentatively, warily he opened an eye to see his inquisitor sitting where he had been before, wearing that same bland, impassive look on his face. Several seconds passed, and still there was no change in Por's expression. A look of puzzlement leaped from Jimmy's open eye across to the other, hoisting the lid and eyebrow almost simultaneously. The seconds grew into interminable minutes, and the longer they stretched the more Jimmy became tight-lipped and embarrassed.

He was about to stutter some inconsequentiality, (like 'Pardon me but is there a toilet around here?' or 'I didn't mean to send you to sleep, but could you tell me when the next meal is?'), when he was startled by a low rumble coming from somewhere between Por's chest and throat. It grew gradually until it burst from his body, a continuous stream of words which didn't mean an awful lot to the boys. What made Jimmy's mouth gape even further was the way in which the words tumbled from Por's mouth. His lips were entirely still and fast shut!

This state continued for several minutes, with the boys understanding nothing until the last few sentences cut through their consciousness like a stab of intense light. Not only were they slower in tempo, but they were said in the language Jimmy and Tommy understood.

> *"If no moon along thou see'st*
> *Upon the Eve of Doran's Feast*
>
> *The Fortress shall return again*
> *Twixt Point and Wood of Linden.*
>
> *If the Orb shines outward bright*
> *Thou must await a year this night.*
>
> *The Seth is mighty in his power.*
> *Hasten not his glorious hour.*
>
> *His victory will be swift and sure*
> *And shall endure for evermore."*

The chant stopped abruptly as Por's eyes once more returned to normal.

"Tomorrow is the Feast of Doran," he said simply.

Chapter Eleven

"Now what?" muttered Tommy to his brother, scratching his head with a puzzled frown on his face. "Mum's not going to like this one little bit. You know how she fusses if you're even a little bit late, and here we are waiting for something we are not sure is ever going to happen."

"But…but …" Jimmy blurted out defensively, his bottom lip beginning to quiver slightly, "it's not my fault. I didn't ask to come here in the first place. I'm beginning to wish I was back home with mum's bossiness. I wish … I wish Uncle Reuben was here. He'd know how to get us back."

The resultant crash of thunder took them completely by surprise.

"Oh no!" muttered Tommy again. "That's all we need! We'd better get out of this clearing and under those trees. Jimmy…?"

His brother did not answer. His feet were immobile, his body swaying slightly, and his face pointing towards something unseen by Tommy.

"Jimmy, are you listening to me?" Tommy hissed. When he still did not answer, Tommy slowly turned his head towards what had caught Jimmy's gaze.

Por had disappeared, but in the gloom beneath the great umbrella of an ancient oak, not fifty paces from their position, they could make out a much deeper shadow. Distinct in outline and nature, the form of the Black Rider and his mighty steed could be picked out, standing motionless save for the occasional flick of a flowing tail, watching, waiting, listening. His great sightless head turned slowly from side to side as if to sense what he couldn't see, when, as suddenly as he had appeared, the Rider swung himself into the unseen saddle. The beast reared momentarily, pawing the air with huge prancing feet, and was gone, leaving its rumour amongst the lowermost branches of the surrounding trees.

"Cor!" sighed Jimmy. "Did you see what I saw?"

"Yes!" gasped his brother. "But he didn't see us. Did you see his face? No face!"

"I wonder where Por's got to," muttered Jimmy, beginning to take the many strange happenings as commonplace. "He seems to have disappeared. When do we eat? I'm hungry. My stomach thinks eating's gone out of fashion."

No sooner had the words tumbled out from his lips than a tinkling silver trumpet sounded somewhere off to their left by the same oak umbrella which sheltered the Black Rider. As the boys spun round wondering where the noise was coming from and what it signalled, a large green-clad man stepped out from underneath the oak tree and beckoned to them. Looking at each other and shrugging, they had no choice but to follow.

Once around the tree, they entered what could only be described as a room in the round with walls of living trees. Their boles were so close together, allowing hardly space enough for a squirrel or even a spider to pass between. At one end of the 'living room', which was quite large by ordinary standards, was a huge table sawn from some enormous tree stump which had long since been felled by one of the frequent violent storms, natural or otherwise, which sweep the area. Upon this table was set a vast array of the choicest foods a boy could wish to fix his eyes on.

"Sit and eat as you will," a deep voice boomed close by. They both jumped at the unexpected interruption. Por had returned, unseen, a slight smile playing around the corners of his mouth.

Much to their undoubted joy and satisfaction the meal seemed endless. When their stomachs finally felt as if they would sink through the floor, and they thought they would never need to eat again, ever, Por began to speak.

"We made a slight misinterpretation of the Rhyme of Doran earlier," he began.

"Do you mean…?" Jimmy interrupted.

"That we won't get the parcel after all?" finished Tommy.

"No, indeed," Por continued. "The Feast of Doran is not tomorrow as we first thought…"

"Oh no!" Tommy burst out in frustration, realising his mum would still be waiting for an explanation as to why he hadn't returned sooner.

"It's tonight!" Por went on.

"Oh heck!" Jimmy joined in, not really knowing why he had done so, other than to let everyone know that he was still there.

"Does that really matter?" Tommy asked again. "I mean, can't we do tonight what we would have done tomorrow?"

"There are two difficulties," Por tried to explain. "One: for the Castle of Seth to appear in the appointed way there has to be no moon. As you see, we are into late afternoon with clear, cloudless skies. Two: we are some twenty leagues south of the usual sighting, with only three hours to the feast."

"Can't we catch a bus...or...something?" Jimmy interrupted, realising at once how silly that question was. Feeling the same embarrassment he had experienced in Oompah's Castle, he thrust his hands even deeper into his pockets, shuffled about a bit, and generally wished he wasn't there.

The inevitable questions about 'bus' did not come flooding to Jimmy's ears as one might have expected on hearing a word not before encountered. In fact, not only did Por *not* ask about Jimmy's mistake, he positively *ignored* the whole subject; a matter of great surprise.

"Our only way," Por continued, oblivious to Jimmy's comments or embarrassment, "is on foot."

Jimmy gulped that gulp of disbelief, which is often accompanied by a nervous laugh. He looked at Tommy for some sign that it wasn't so, but all he could do was shrug his shoulders and look again at Por, who by this time was watching them intently.

"OK, then," the boys chorused steadily. "When do we start?"

"We have just done so," the Chieftain of the Wandering People replied.

This puzzled the brothers, until Jimmy looked up, and his jaw began to creep slowly to meet his chest.

Jimmy's mouth opened and closed slowly in a

reasonable impersonation of a goldfish in its bowl, not quite believing what he saw. He watched the trees and shrubbery they had been standing in, beginning to thin out quite considerably, moving past them in a constant stream, like the countryside slips by when you are on a bus or something, but more slowly.

Tommy thought he had seen all there was to see and met with all the surprises this world had to offer, so he was stunned by this latest magic. All Jimmy could do was watch in open-mouthed disbelief, and say "Coo!" like an absent-minded pigeon.

"But…but…!" stammered Tommy after a few moments incredulity. "It's moving! The wood's moving and…we're not!" There was a look of panic almost in his face as he rounded on Por.

"Do not be afraid," reassured Por. "We travel thus at need. Not for nought is the forest so named. However, only in the forest is it possible. Once outside its eaves, we must adopt a more standard means of transport as our 'magic', I think you call it, is proof only under our roof. This way we cover many leagues with the least delay.

"However, when our northernmost eaves reach us, we will still have several leagues left to go, across open country. It is there we will need all our craft and guile to bring us through. Even then, it is by no means certain Seth will oblige us with an appearance. Treachery is his art, and we should expect no less. He knows by now what is your mission, and he will try all at his disposal to stop you. The only thing he doesn't know is where your parcel is hidden. Should he take you…?"

The sudden silence left the boys in no doubt as to their fate or the fate of the whole universe, should Seth be successful in *his* quest.

The time passed reasonably quickly and even though there were many interesting and unusual things which caught their eyes, Jimmy became inevitably bored by it all, and began to shuffle. It *was* rather a long time for a little boy to stand, waiting without shuffling, and besides, he was beginning to get pins and needles in his left foot. By the time the numbness had crept halfway up his leg, his eyes were beginning to hurt from the constant streaming past.

Suddenly, without any warning at all, the journey stopped. It took several minutes for Jimmy's eyeballs to stop moving in sympathy, but stop they did, only to be assaulted by that red sun again. Behind them crouched the mysterious brooding presence of the forest, and before them, the river which flashed like a silver ribbon, curling around the forest to be lost behind its hazy shadow.

Across the river, stretching interminably towards an enormous outcrop of jagged rocks, lay a wide featureless plain, broken only by an occasional copse of weathered trees. Beyond the crags, only just on the limits of vision even in this clear rarefied air, was a tower, the like of which they had never seen before. Its very rumour struck fear and foreboding into the stoutest heart.

"Tom," hissed Jimmy, "looks like we've got company." He nodded towards the eaves of the wood they had just travelled with, where several very large beings, garbed in brown and green, were standing.

"I'd not seen them before," Tom answered. "Have you seen their size? They must be at least seven feet tall! I wonder …"

"They are the Guard," Por's voice broke in. "Fearless,

fierce in combat, and virtually invincible, we shall doubtless need them before the night is over. The prospect is good, I feel. Look! Cloud is building from the north and should blanket the heavens before nightfall."

"What's that building?" Tommy asked. "I mean, the one over there on the horizon."

Por's eyes narrowed and his mouth set into a hard line. A long, slow, soft hiss issued from his body as he filled his lungs, gathering himself to speak. There was a pause, full of expectancy and foreboding; a pause of reluctance and indecision.

"Many lives of men old," he started, "its foundations were laid by the lore masters of old as a guardian to the northernmost reaches of this land. Before the walls had been raised evil forces overthrew the Wardens and it wasn't until much later, when the evil ones had raised it to its present pinnacle, that we realised Seth had long held designs on it. He secretly occupied it and fortified it through the sorrow of many Omnians. Its power is now lessened because it is under the powerful and watchful eye of the Guardian of Omni..."

"We've heard a lot about him," Jimmy interrupted. "Who is he? Why can't he get rid of Seth and set everything to rights?"

"And why can't the world be made in a day and all the rivers flow uphill?" smiled Por. "Seth's power has grown great; great even by the standards of the ancient masters. The power in this land is founded upon the very bones of Omni and is more ancient than the world itself. It is enough - just. He is one whom we call Thenomni, Master of All, commonly known as Algan."

"Algan!" burst out Tommy. "But, we've already met

him. It was he who sent us. We've been into the Enchanted Cave."

"Then fortunate you are indeed," Por said with surprise. "Few have ever done so. There is more to you than meets the eye, I can see."

"Is it much further now? Are we there yet?" Jimmy asked wearily. "My feet are tired." He sank to the ground, exhausted, as the smoky dusk began to creep into the surrounding area and the shadows deepened under the eaves of the forest. They had travelled now some league and a half since leaving the forest, always with the River Lin on their right hand side, and always within sight and reach.

"We need go no further," Por answered. "You are tired, I can see. We are here."

Chapter Twelve

The early evening passed slowly and uneasily, with a profound sense of disquiet falling over the whole area. Even the usually immovable Por seemed ill at ease as if waiting for some final blow of doom to fall. The only beings seemingly unmoved by the scene were the Guard, who stood in a semi-circle around their leader, three paces apart, motionless, save for the slight breeze movement of their shoulder-length hair.

All animal and bird activity and noise had long since ceased, as if they too were watching, waiting. Tired as he was, Jimmy had simply curled up where he had fallen and was now sleeping that deep, innocent sleep of the young, untroubled by the uncertain times and events he now found himself party to. What uncertain part he had to play in the final scene, if any, was as yet unclear to anyone there. All they knew was that the hammer was about to fall, perhaps to crush all under its evil blow.

"Jim! Jim!" hissed Tommy. "Wake up! Something's happening."

"Umph," Jimmy replied, jerking out of a pleasant fireside chat at his Uncle Reuben's. He could have sworn he *really was* in Omni, his uncle's tale had been so vivid. The reality suddenly dawned on him with that hard tussock of plains grass biting into his neck.

"What is it?" he yawned. "What's happening?"

"Look!" Tommy whispered. "The night is pitch, but the clouds are breaking, and can you feel that...that...silence?"

Jimmy's gaze drifted up to the ominous gathered storm clouds to see, in truth, that they were being shredded and dispersed by a stiff breeze. The river had also changed dramatically. From the placid, glinting, gentle ribbon, it had become a disturbed raging animal with foam-capped wavelets lapping angrily at the banks, threatening to pull them into the torrent.

The Guard stiffened visibly as Por forced out his words against the now-howling gale.

"The moment is at hand," he gasped. "Seth's hour is nigh. If the clouds can hold but a moment or two longer it will all be finished."

"Look! Look!" cried Tommy, battling against the wind to remain upright. "The clouds!"

All gazes shot upwards to see that the last vestiges of cloud had disappeared to reveal - no moon!

At that precise moment, the ground was shaken by an almighty quake, which knocked over all but the Guard. The forest trees were caught by a blast of wind so fierce that their outer guardians were uprooted and scattered like a handful of harvest chaff.

Jimmy was knocked senseless momentarily, but on regaining consciousness, he found himself straddled by two enormous green and brown tree trunks. The only thought to find substance in his head was that these didn't look like tree trunks at all, more like...legs! On looking up to the topmost branches he found that they *were* legs - those of a Guard bracing himself for battle. There he stayed in the relative safety of his guardian, watching in awed amazement as the scene before him unravelled.

Stone upon stone, battlement upon impregnable battlement, a castle of immeasurable strength grew out of the bare treeless earth. In as little time as it takes to say it, the stronghold was completed, pinnacle-topped towers crowned with stiff breezeless black pennants and drawbridge firmly shut. Where there had been an uninterrupted view across open plain to the Craggs of Gotts Point, now menaced castle, stagnant moat and thickly wooded surrounds.

"That's it!" gasped Jimmy. "The tree! The split tree I put the parcel in! It's there by the moat!" His arm shook as he stabbed his finger into the gloom, towards the tree, and without hesitation, he scrambled to his feet and launched himself towards his goal. Had it not been for Por's restraining arm, he would have leaped forward into the jaws of hell.

"Not yet, my boy," he whispered. "We go together."

As one, warily in the eerie silence surrounding the castle, they moved forward a few paces into the undergrowth. Great stealth was needed to arouse as little commotion as possible. Moving from copse to copse, and thicket to thicket, they came to within twenty-five paces of the parcel's hiding place. Por made a sign for Jimmy and his brother to carry on to retrieve their parcel. As Uncle Reuben had entrusted it to him, Jimmy had felt it was his responsibility to get it back.

They hesitated, gulped twice and launched themselves forward, making sure no-one was watching.

"This is easy," whispered Tommy as they neared the

tree. "Go on, take it. I can see it sticking out by the base."

As Jimmy reached out to take his prize, his ears were filled with that same dreaded rattle and high-pitched scream which had seemingly stabbed a cold blade through his heart previously. He swung around to find the surrounding area covered with their evil white sightless bodies.

The Senti were abroad, driven on by their merciless master. The boys, swinging left and right at them until their arms ached with the exertion, slowly succumbed to the sheer weight of numbers. They were about to submerge totally under the foul sea, when the welcome sound of ringing trumpets and the crack of blade against body surged to Jimmy's ears. The Guard were wading thigh deep through the ranks of Senti, tossing them aside like sheaves of corn at a harvest. Por's double-edged axe whistled and sang in its tireless quest to rid the world of its enemy.

Suddenly, the brothers were relieved of their irksome living blanket by two enormous hands plucking them from the masses.

"The parcel!" yelled Jimmy in terror. "It's gone! One of them has taken it!"

The Guardsman had set down its charge and it shot off in hot pursuit of a black-cloaked Senti that wore a grey circlet around its head. Fortunately for Jimmy, the creature didn't move very quickly, hampered as it was by its cloak and its lack of vision. He soon drew level with its shambling body, with Tommy only a stride behind, and despite the creature's shrieks for aid, he took it in the cleanest rugby tackle ever seen outside of Twickenham, with Tommy tumbling on top and grabbing the parcel at the same time. The last view he had of Omni was the Black Rider marshalling the forces of the river in row upon row of foam-capped wave riders, breaking on the disordered ranks of Senti and sweeping them away to their destruction. A split second afterwards, the lights went out as the Faceless Rider flung his cloak of darkness over the scene of battle.

Chapter Thirteen

"Tommy," came a whispered voice somewhere nearby, "where are we? I can't see anything in this fog. It is foggy, isn't it?"

"Yes, it is foggy," came the reply, "and I don't know where we are. Have you still got the parcel?"

"Yes, it's under my arm," Jimmy said, after a moment or two's hesitation. "Which way do we go? I don't ... what was that?"

The younger boy stopped, his eyes peering into the clinging gloom, trying to put an object to the noise he had heard.

"There it goes again!" he continued.

"Yes, I heard it that time," Tommy agreed. "It sounds like ... like ... voices, whispering."

"Hello ... who's there?" Jimmy's voice quavered with more than a little fear. The whispers continued and grew gradually in number and intensity until they were surrounded by a constant wheezy, hissing noise like the air escaping from two or three dozen leaky bagpipes.

"I don't like this at all," Tommy observed.

"I wish we were at home," whined Jimmy, somewhat put off. "Tom, are you still there?"

Silence. No answer.

"Tom," urged Jimmy, a note of panic rising in his throat. "Tom, answer me ..."

"Shut up a minute!" came Tommy's voice from the other side of his brother. "I'm trying to hear what they are saying."

"You are in the Foggy Land of Four," wheezed a voice almost inaudibly.

"Who are you?" Tommy asked, not really expecting to get a reply.

"We are the Long-undead," came the whispered reply after a short pause. "We, like you, were caught in travel before the time strands parted to let us through. You will stay here."

"Not on your life!" yelled Jimmy. "My mum's waiting and my tea'll be ready by now. I *can't* stay, thank you very much."

With that, he struggled forward as well as he could, which wasn't very well. They seemed to be held by a thick blanket of foam, making walking rather like trying to swim through a lake of treacle. As the voices grew in volume and clarity, so too were the boys able to see what forms were making the sounds. The faces and forms closing in on them were those of old, grey and haggard people with grasping fingers, coming ever nearer. They tried to move but couldn't. They were trapped! They would become Whispering Voices like all the others!

The ghostly forms, not a foot away from them, and now clearly defined, were about to grasp the hapless boys when they were blinded by the intensity of brilliant sunlight - *yellow* sunlight! The boys were relieved to feel gravel under their feet and the scent of lavender in their nostrils - Reuben's garden; they were in Reuben's garden!

Jimmy spun round on his heels to catch sight of a small, silver-handled door slowly closing in the fence, with a rapidly dispersing carpet of mist on the soil before it. Jimmy gulped, looked across at Tommy, then turned again to find the fence was just a fence, and they were home.

"Well now, old chaps," came a deep, familiar voice from behind them. "Back I see."

It was Uncle Reuben.

"Are we glad to see you, Uncle!" Tommy blurted out.

"We were nearly gonners in there!" Jimmy joined in.

"Did you ever doubt you'd get back?" Uncle Reuben asked, the same smile playing around his mouth. "Had an adventure or two, I'll be bound!"

"This parcel certainly…" Jimmy started, looking down at his hands.

"But it's not there!" he went on. "I could have sworn I brought it back! Did Seth…?"

Uncle Reuben shook his head slowly, smiled even more, and winked a long, slow wink which both silenced any further questions and told the boys all they wanted to know.

"Tea and ice cream are on the table," he went on. "Come on, we can talk later."

"That cherry cake was good," said Tommy still mentally licking his lips on the top deck of the bus home.

"I wonder what mum'll say," Jimmy mused. "Do you think she'll be cross?"

"She will to start with," replied Tommy, "but she'll mellow. She always does."

Silence fell over the two boys. They were alone on the top deck, with only the rattle of the engine and clanking of the cracked bell for company.

"What do you make of this?" Jimmy asked his brother after several minutes' fumbling in the inside pocket of his anorak. Slowly, and very gingerly, he pulled out a grey circlet, the circumference of which was a little greater than his two fists.

"Where on earth did you get that from?" Tommy gasped. "That's the head circlet of that boss Senti who nearly got your parcel!"

"Yes, I know," sighed Jimmy. "I grabbed him as the time strands cracked, and he sort of seemed to come with me into the Foggy Land of Four, but then he disappeared. Shall I throw it away?"

"Not on your life!" exclaimed his brother. "Keep it. It might come in useful - one day."

They had been so engrossed in their conversation that they didn't see their stop loom up and begin to recede until Tommy grabbed his brother and hurtled down the stairs and on to the pavement. They ambled along the pavement and up the front path of their house, not really wishing to be met by mum's initial outburst. It had been known to put out the fire across the room it was so violent.

Tommy, being the bigger of the two, pushed Jimmy through the front door ahead of him. He tried, in vain, to turn and regain the door, but the hall was too narrow and a shrill voice stopped him in his tracks.

"Hello, boys," came the voice.

It was mum.

Both boys expected the usual "and where do you think you've been?"

Jimmy nudged Tommy to say something and he looked most uncomfortable whilst mumbling his apologies.

"Er, sorry we're a bit late mum," he muttered, "but we sort of got held up. You see…"

"How do you mean 'late'?" she asked, rather puzzled. "This is your usual time home from school."

School? Tommy shot a profoundly puzzled look across at his brother who shrugged his shoulders and looked back at his mum.

"What's the matter with you two?" she asked again. "You should be happy. You're usually much more cheerful than this on the last day of a school term. Come on, brighten up, it's the first day of your holiday tomorrow."

Jimmy's jaw slowly but surely sagged until it nearly ended in his coat top pocket. Had it all been one long fantastic dream?

He was beginning to doubt, when his fingers strayed onto the circlet, deep in his pocket…

Tea was something of a subdued and quiet affair with their mother enquiring after their health because of their silence. Jimmy didn't seem to have much time to reflect with his family constantly on top of him. Very quickly this little house had become so claustrophobic, shut in, and inert after the activity, excitement, and open space he had experienced in Omni. He still couldn't understand how they could have 'lost' all that time whilst there; something to do with somebody called 'Einstein' Tommy had mumbled through a mouthful of food once mum was out of the room. He'd no idea who *he* was at any rate, and conversation was so stilted and hurried as mum flitted in and out at crucial points of their discussion. So they drifted into an uneasy silence. Perhaps they might get the chance to talk at bed time.

"Well, what do you think about that?" Jimmy asked Tommy in a hushed whisper, in their shared room, that night.

"Think about what?" Tommy replied absent-mindedly once in their bedroom, genuinely seeming to be oblivious as to what he was talking about. Jimmy was surprised and annoyed that Tommy could put on this front of almost confused ignorance, when he knew full well what Jimmy was talking about.

"Why do you do that?" Jimmy asked, with barely suppressed annoyance. "You know what I mean! Omni; what do you make of what happened to us earlier today?"

"Oh, that!" Tommy answered, dismissively, whilst paying greater attention to his Gameboy than to what Jimmy wanted him to say. "Just another day out, really. I think you need to accept it for what it was – another day out – and move on. It's not going to happen again; it was a one off, and I'm not sure what happened at all. Now, if you don't mind …"

Jimmy usually knew his brother quite well, and he remembered that he could be awkward and unco-operative, but this wasn't like him at all. Why was he being so off-hand and non-committal? Could it be that he was finding, at his grand old age of thirteen, that it was all a bit too much to take in and that he was feeling a bit overwhelmed by what they had experienced, or was he just a little bit embarrassed by the whole fantasy of it all? Generally, Tommy was not given to fantasy, being a sporty and a practical person, and this current attitude might be his reaction to what he usually called "airy-fairy" stuff. Jimmy realised that there would be no gain from pursuing *his* line of thought, and, disappointed that he wouldn't be able to share their experience, he decided he would have to work through it all by himself.

The following days saw Jimmy spending much more time on his own, and Tommy disappearing off "somewhere" with his mates, all of whom had been to the same school as Jimmy and had known him since he was *able* to be known. However, to them he had become almost persona non grata, probably because of Tommy's attitude, and the fact that *they* were teenagers who did not associate with anyone so young.

Jimmy spent such a long time on his own with no-one to share the experiences with, he began to internalise more of his thoughts and feelings to such an extent that he spent hours each day in sometimes deep reveries. Once here, it became increasingly difficult for his mother to cajole or even threaten him out of them. Of course, he spent much of his time mentally in Omni, where the sights, sounds and smells evoked the more exciting and adventurous periods of his recent young life.

He walked with the Wandering People under the dappling shade of the Shifting Forest, where he was happy to be confused by the ever-changing pathways and undergrowths. He even imagined that headlong fall to oblivion he almost experienced the first time he encountered Great Gaping Ghyll, taking him further and further within himself.

Sometimes he allowed his consciousness to be invaded by the living nightmare, of when Seth interrogated him endlessly in his stronghold; excruciatingly, mind-probingly frightening, but all part of the day dreaming which was in danger of taking over his life. The peril in this was for him to 'live' in Omni so much that he would find great difficulty separating fantasy from reality, and for one so young, that *could* spell disaster.

For mum, the one redeeming feature of this interminably long summer holiday was its end, an end which promised, she hoped, a solution to Jimmy's day dreaming inattention. That game at the Last Chance saloon would come in the form of a return to school, and the care of his teacher, Mr Bolam. He had always been good for Jimmy, had Mr Bolam, keeping him from wasting his talents which, throughout his school career, might have been squandered had it not been for Mr Bolam. She hoped beyond all hope that it wouldn't be too late, and that school would be the cure for this growing concern she held.

Chapter Fourteen

"Scoggins! Jimmy Scoggins!" sighed Mr Bolam, his transparent patience allowing a tangible irritation to peek through. "*Now* where have you been? I've seen nothing but the whites of your eyes, and the inside of your eyelids since we came back from the summer holiday. Scoggins!"

The last riposte shot from his lips and struck Jimmy's eardrums like a ricocheting bullet. This time the result was startling. Jimmy Scoggins jerked his head backwards from his supporting hands, and the two chair legs he was balancing on became none, spread-eagling him on the threadbare classroom carpet tiles between his desk and Peter Chambers' in the row behind.

The ensuing uproar from his classmates brought a resigned hands-on-hips stance, and a look of capitulating resignation from his teacher.

This had been the continuation of a deep reverie, which had started mid-way through the holiday, and had interrupted frequently his every waking hour. The only peace he had from it were his hours of unconsciousness in bed, where his mind was entirely blank, or so he thought.

Constantly, the very real images of Omni, and his adventures there, infiltrated his days wherever he was, whatever he was doing. Sometimes they were wondrous, taking him to the highest pinnacles of breathless excitement. Other times, he wished they would go away and leave him alone to become an ordinary boy again. This, unfortunately, was not going to happen any time soon.

"Mr Scoggins, either pay attention to your work, my words, and this lesson, or I will send you to explain yourself to the headmaster," Mr Bolam interrupted his thoughts again, this time with more than a little real annoyance in his tone.

It was at times such as this, and other confrontational occasions that Jimmy's hand strayed to the Senti circlet he always kept in his pocket. Touching this somehow seemed to settle his confidence, as he felt a slight surge of power course through his body. Whilst he had no desire to show defiance towards his teacher's insistence, he did feel able to weather any storm, which might gather about him.

He bowed his head and pretended to concentrate on the work in front of him, but images of his time in Omni at best flashed past his inner eye, and at worst flooded his consciousness. To his teacher, Jimmy's daydreaming, whilst an irritant and nuisance before the summer holidays, was now becoming a serious problem; a problem which would need attention sooner rather than later.

A sudden sharp pain to the side of his head just behind the ear, dredged Jimmy out of his reverie. It wasn't a Senti barb but a wet, rolled piece of paper, which stuck momentarily to his head and then slithered from his shoulder onto his book, causing a wet stain to ooze into what little writing he had accomplished. A reflex action clapped his hand to his head, drawing sniggers from two boys two rows away. Jimmy swung around to catch that evil smirk on the face of Dwayne Davis, the class bully, who had decided that it was time he paid Jimmy Scoggins some attention.

Dwayne Davis was that perennial classical bully who found delight only in causing discomfiture to those smaller than himself. Large for his age by any standard, his bulbous body was topped by a round, deeply freckled face, which was framed in bright ginger spikes, shaved close to the head above the ears. No one ever challenged him, or complained to the teachers, because they were afraid of size and consequence. Jimmy had always shied away from contact, and had stayed off Dwayne's radar, until now. Because of the constant attention he received through his inattention, Jimmy's blip had suddenly appeared on Dwayne Davis' screen.

The act of unwarranted aggression, along with a covertly shaken fist had a strange effect on Jimmy. That directionless, daydreaming mind, which, like a rudderless Senti, had drifted aimlessly on a sea of inaction, now acquired sharp focus. The fuzziness in his brain, which had plagued his every conscious hour, dissipated as the mist at noon on an early autumn day. This was behaviour no longer to be tolerated.

"OK everybody," Mr Bolam said, "time for break. Pack everything away and line up at the door."

The general excited hubbub of a classroom of ten year olds preparing for freedom, if only for fifteen minutes, in an otherwise busy day, was surprisingly muted. The day was bright and sunny and would allow them to run off some of that pent-up energy most children of that age possess in profusion. In the line at the door, the engine was ticking over ready for that tap on the accelerator which would allow the machine to surge into life. Fifteen minutes at full throttle would be enough to burn off some of that high octane activity, to allow them to sustain another hour and a half's physical inactivity before lunch time's next energy burst.

The bully Dwayne and his buddy Billy were at the head of the line, having shouldered their way in whilst Mr Bolam's back was turned. Billy Jones was a much smaller boy than Dwayne; shifty-looking with close-cropped black hair, who had not been any trouble in school until the middle of the previous year. This had coincided with his association with now-bosom-buddy Dwayne. Billy had suffered at the hands of bullies in his previous school, so his policy had been actively to seek out the bully in his present school, curry favour, and play a supporting if minor role. This would ensure protection both from Dwayne and from any other like-minded thugs. Their being the first out into the playground would allow them to pick off Jimmy as he emerged.

As he set foot over the threshold, a hard thwack to the back of the head from a rolled comic caught him off-balance, and pitched him forward onto his hands and knees, grazing both. Jimmy was up in an instant, to an attempted guffaw from his now childish antagonists. Expecting a follow-up, Jimmy spun on his heels, ducked under the anticipated wild swing, and delivered a sharp kick to Dwayne's knee. The result was startling, if somewhat unexpected. A tearing screech destroyed the surrounding airs, rather reminiscent of the boss Senti when Jimmy relieved it of its circlet, as Dwayne collapsed to the ground clutching his knee. Billy remained rooted, fear swimming in his eyes, expecting the same treatment.

Jimmy stood up, fists clenched, but on seeing Dwayne's

demise he relaxed, straightened his back, and held both Dwayne and Billy with his eyes. The fat bully stopped squealing, and rose unsteadily to his feet. The playground noise gradually faded away, and all movement from the other children slowed as if all action had been paused. Even birds stopped in mid-flight, and smoke from nearby chimneys came to a halt. The three boys were the only ones moving in real time, as Jimmy rounded on the other two. Not a word did he utter as he engaged their minds.

"Your bullying ways *will* stop!" he commanded in a way, which left their minds in no doubt about the consequences of disobedience. As the two bullies shrank away from him, Jimmy seemed to grow in stature both mentally and physically. "From now," Jimmy's mind continued, "you will bully no one else. If you disobey, retribution will be swift and harsh. I call on a higher power to be my witness." His thoughts boomed in their heads, strengthening their resolve to mend their ways.

Jimmy's power waned in the same way it had waxed moments earlier, and slowly the playground once more became a playground, with youngsters darting around, completely oblivious to the drama that had just unfolded within their midst.

Although the two boys remained huddled together near the entrance to school, which is what they usually did anyway, Jimmy was nowhere to be seen.

Reuben sat upright in the great chair of his study, gloom gathering about him. Although still bright and piercing, his eyes were distant, as if gazing at a scene which was almost at the edge of vision. The gloom slowly deepened as storm clouds gathered above him, and a profound chill began to creep outwards from the great globe on his desk. It took only a few minutes for the gloom to envelop everything except for what had become the faintly glowing outline of one of the tapestries of Omni, and Reuben himself.

Almost imperceptibly, the confines of the room gave way to a hilltop covered in grassy heath tussocks, the chair became a fallen tree stump, and the chill had grown steadily to become a knee-deep, icy mist. It was as if Reuben had become part of the tapestry. Was it by his design? Or had he been summoned? The clouds above him gathered ominously, not for the weather they might bring, but for another different onslaught they might unleash.

Ostensibly in a trance, Reuben did not move. The slight breeze disturbed his shock of black curls only slightly, as his half-moon spectacles reflected the warm autumn sunshine. Impassive, almost dispassionate, his intense blue eyes flashed momentarily into life, displaying a depth of activity that belied his physical inactivity. Ordinary, everyday creatures within a huge radius of Reuben's hill, slowly ceased to move. Autumnal leaves stopped mid-fall. Everything became still, except for Reuben's breeze-disturbed hair. The gloom closed in until only his slightly glowing face could be seen.

"So you are here to confront me at last," the voice grew slowly in Reuben's mind. "Do you feel you can at last challenge the Seth? What you must ask yourself is how will *your* meagre powers, such as they are, stand up to *my* powers which are limitless, and born of the very bones of this land?"

126

Reuben's eyes flashed, as his mind surged without saying anything. *That* surge revealed a fraction of the strength that was Reuben; a revelation, which made Seth recoil slightly, showing that Reuben's power was to be neither ignored nor dismissed.

"The upstart feels he may be able to challenge me, does he?" mocked Seth. "You, I will deal with in due time. More pressing is the young bearer of the parcel, who shall feel the full onslaught of my wrath for his temerity in meddling in affairs which do not concern him. Bear in mind that I know where I can find Master Scoggins, so that I might pay him a visit at any time, soon."

"You will not have your way, Master of Despair," rejoined Reuben sharply.

"You *do* possess a voice, oh leader of your band of ragamuffins and ne'er-do-wells!" Seth taunted.

"...And a voice that will resonate in your mind as it dominates all you hold dear!" snarled Reuben, dismissing Seth's rejoinder with utter contempt.

Seth was silenced and taken aback somewhat by the intensity of the riposte, which was delivered as a rapier opens up an opponent's defences.

"As far as my "ragamuffins" are concerned," Reuben continued with renewed vigour, "should you attempt to do them harm, your fall will be so swift and so low, never in this age of the world will the Evil Lord of Seth be seen again."

"Empty words, old man," Seth replied, but without much conviction, a doubt growing ever greater in his mind such power did he feel from Reuben. "You will never be strong enough, with your entire rabble, to overcome the Seth!" and with that, he was gone.

With the disappearance of Seth, the mist cloud and gloom began to dissipate, the breeze and wildlife in the countryside came alive slowly once again, and a lark started to send out its beautiful, fluid notes as it spiralled upwards, on its way to its place in the upper airs, imbuing all who could hear it with a sense of gladness and hope.

The waxing of Jimmy's Omnian will with his dealings with Dwayne and Billy, carried him back fleetingly to that glorious place. As if to reaffirm that he now belonged to that realm, and to reawaken the resolve which had carried him through many dangerous adventures.

Immediately he landed, he knew where he was. There was no mistaking the southern-most eaves of the Shifting Forest of Linden. Its shimmering and sighing leaf-dressed branches offered sanctuary from the unusually warm sun. Somehow the forest seemed to know why you were there and what you needed to make your life as comfortable as you wished it to be. Jimmy's mind ran back to the first time he had encountered the forest, during that first parcel visit to Omni. He remembered also that it was almost his last visit – anywhere. He wouldn't be renewing his acquaintance with the Great Gaping Ghyll *this* time – he hoped!

A thought struck him. Why was he here? Shouldn't he have been somewhere else? Somewhere entirely different? School! Playtime? Dwayne Davis!

A movement, which was not tree-related, he caught out of the corner of his eye. People? No, surely not! There it was again! They were beings of some sort, he felt sure. But what were they? They *seemed* to be humanoid, perhaps half-size, but had a translucence about them, which made them difficult to see entirely. Although, having been involved with the working of Linden twice before, this could have been an illusion the forest wished to create.

Yes, that was definitely – the bell for the end of playtime! The trees and gentle wafting breeze had given way to hard-edged walls, a paint-peeling door, and dozens of clapping feet and squealing voices. He was back in school! This *was* the same school, only it *felt* different, somehow. It was more clearly defined, the fuzzy-edges had disappeared, and he felt, at least for the time being, that he belonged here.

"Nice of you to join us, Mr Scoggins," came that sarcasm he recognised so well as he closed the classroom door behind him. All his classmates were in and settled to Mr Bolam's maths lesson.

"Please sit down and have the goodness to join the lesson," he added more sharply. "I'm sure you won't want to complete what you have missed after school this afternoon."

"Sorry, Mr Bolam," Jimmy answered with a certain confidence and authority. "It won't happen again."

The teacher was a little taken aback by this answer, but returned to the point of the lesson.

At the end of this session, as all the children were leaving to line up for lunch, Mr Bolam asked Jimmy to remain behind. Jimmy's performance in this particular class had improved immeasurably. The change puzzled the teacher so much that he wanted answers.

"OK," he started, "who are you, and where have you hidden the *real* Jimmy Scoggins?"

"I don't follow, sir," Jimmy answered, rather confused.

"My obviously unsuccessful attempt at humour!" Mr Bolam explained. "Before break, and even since the summer holidays, you have been 'elsewhere'. You have done no work whatsoever, and I have wasted a lot of my time trying to 'find' you. And now ..." he shrugged " ... you have – what can I say... dominated the most un-favourite of all your subjects? Your work this lesson has been nothing short of – inspired. Why? How?"

Jimmy thought for a few seconds, not able to explain the real reason, and then he said quite simply, "I really don't know, sir. Before, I seemed to have been in a dream that I can't explain. The only explanation I can give is that it's like that Bible story you told us last term about Saul on his way to Damascus, you know, the one where he was struck by light, and later changed his attitude, and understood. I didn't understand it then, but I do now."

Mr Bolam was stunned. He didn't know what to say, and so simply dismissed the boy with a lame "I hope it continues" comment. However, from now on he would pay greater attention to young Jimmy Scoggins, and to his progress.

"Jimmy! Jimmy Scoggins!" came a little voice from behind him in the dinner queue. Jimmy turned sharply but could see no one he might know.

"It's me, Peter Lee," insisted the voice. "I'm back here."

Jimmy isolated the voice finally, five people behind him in the queue. It issued from a thin, fair-haired boy of about eight or nine, with an excited and expectant look on his face.

"Can I come and sit with you when I've got me dinner?" Peter asked, eyes pleading, as Jimmy turned to get his mash and fish fingers.

"It's a free country," Jimmy said. "Do whatever makes you happy." He turned away, walking slowly so that the moat of thin brown gravy around the mound of mash on his plate would not escape either down his shirt or onto his shoe. He chose an empty table in the corner of the hall by the window, giving a vista onto the school playing field and the hills beyond. He had enacted many an adventure in those hills, before he discovered Omni.

"How did you do that?" Peter blurted out as he set his plate on the table next to Jimmy's.

"Do what?" Jimmy returned, a little puzzled.

"You know, stopped that bully Davis and his sidekick Billy Jones after they, he, attacked you at playtime," Peter responded eagerly. "One minute you were on the floor; next, Davis was squealing, holding his knee; and then they were slinking into school, quiet and subdued, with you nowhere to be seen. How did you do that?"

"I think you must be mistaken," Jimmy replied guardedly. "I don't remember any of that at all. You sure you didn't imagine it?"

"OK," Peter returned, touching the side of his nose with his index finger, "if you want to keep it to yourself. But can I be your friend?"

"I don't know," Jimmy hesitated.

"Go on," Peter urged. "I'll be a good friend. I've got some wine gums! I know I'm in the year below you, so we can't be classmates, but we can be friends at playtimes, and my Nan lives in your street."

Jimmy knew he would have to be careful not to divulge any of his secrets about Omni, but he saw no harm in being Peter's friend. After all, he didn't really have any others.

All the while Jimmy was having this rather one-sided conversation with Peter, he was being observed from across the room by the sullen and brooding lump that was Dwayne Davis. He had been warned, but perhaps there might be an occasion when he would be able to gain his revenge on Jimmy Scoggins. He would bide his time. He was in no hurry. However, little did he know just how much Jimmy's power was growing, and how fiercely Dwayne's desire for revenge would come back to haunt him.

Jimmy drifted restlessly in and out of consciousness that night. Soon after he had gone to bed, a huge electrical storm developed, which seemed to become entangled with his vivid dreams of Omni, and the strife he and the Omnians had had and were continuing to suffer. The images were so vivid and seemed so real that dreaming and waking could not be distinguished one from the other. The raging battle between people and the elements became overprinted by the stark image of the Faceless Rider, who was no longer faceless. Here he was the prince of a mighty realm, leading battalions of peerless cavalrymen, all clad in shiny black adamantine armour, mounted atop black steeds whose iron-shod hooves struck sparks from the rocks, and whose nostrils snorted fire.

Chapter Fifteen

"Mum?" Jimmy mumbled through a mouthful of Chocoflakes at breakfast.

"If it involves leaving your breakfast to go on some cock-and-bull chase, the answer's no," she replied before he had asked the question, neither breaking routine nor looking up from the washing machine she was loading.

"I wasn't going to ask that," he said defensively. "Do you think it would be all right to visit Uncle Reuben today, seeing as it's Saturday and I haven't been to see him for quite some time?"

"I thought you'd grown out of those visits, and all those silly stories he used to tell you. Childish, Tommy called them," she observed. "Besides, aren't you going to the match with our Tommy?"

"You know I'm not interested in football, and besides, Tom's going with all his mates from secondary school," Jimmy rejoined pointedly. "They don't want me with them."

"Then I don't see why you shouldn't go," she threw back at him from the top step of the back garden, as she began to hang out her first batch of washing to dry. "Perhaps you had better phone him first to make sure he's going to be in. Sorry, forgot he doesn't have a phone, does he?"

Breakfast finished and tidied away, Jimmy wondered

how to get in touch with his uncle, but before he had had the time to decide, the phone rang stridently in his ear, making him jump in surprise.

"Hello?" he asked, rather more tentatively than usual. "Who…?"

"Jim! Old chap!" came that very familiar and welcome voice. "How are you, and where have you been? Long time no see."

"Uncle Reuben!" Jimmy cried, eyes dancing with glee. "I was just wondering about coming to pay you a visit. How did you know?" His uncle never ceased to amaze him. He always seemed to *know* what he was thinking at any given time. Although he was delighted to hear from him, he was a little puzzled to hear him on the telephone at all, given his dislike of the instrument. "But you don't have a phone. So how are you…?"

"Well, don't you know, I borrowed my next door neighbour's, as a matter of simplicity. Could never get used to one of these things," Reuben replied. "I haven't seen my favourite nephew for far too long, and I thought it was time you and I got together, sooner rather than later. How are you fixed for today?"

Jimmy had long since accepted that Reuben was magical, and knew more about *his* business than he would admit to. He felt also that he might be able to answer a few of the more pressing questions about Omni that were troubling his mind.

"That would be fantastic!" Jimmy enthused. "There are some things I would like your advice on."

"Nothing too serious, I hope," Reuben chortled.

"Just one or two … *things* … which are in my head that only you can solve," Jimmy said, dropping almost to a whisper.

"Within the hour suit you?" Reuben asked, and with that, the conversation was over, and Jimmy was out of the front door on his way to the bus stop.

As he reached the gate, two very unusual things happened. Firstly, his bus flew past him a full ten minutes before it was due, empty of passengers and with only a driver and conductor on board. As it reached the end of his street and made to turn the corner into Gemini Road, it slowed and stopped, along with everything else he could see. Mrs Brown's dog stopped in mid-leap after a tennis ball thrown by her son; Jonny French's scarf was still flying out behind his back; and the postman was still pushing hard on his pedals, his letters spilling onto the road as he braked to avoid a cat – all frozen in time.

Jimmy was startled because of his missed bus, and also because this was the second time that this had happened to him in as many days. As he turned to chase the first bus, another one slowly rolled to a halt outside his gate, only this time, there were neither passengers, nor driver, nor conductor. The automatic doors opened, and he found himself urged to board. Well, urged wasn't quite right, because he found he had no choice really; and no sooner had he boarded and the doors had closed, than they were opening again on Tumbles Row – his stop.

He stepped onto the pavement slowly and cautiously to avoid any accident, turned to check he hadn't left anything on his seat, to find the bus was no longer there. Everything around him was slowly returning to real time, unaware of what had happened.

Surprisingly, Jimmy had begun to take unusual and unexpected occurrences in his stride, and as the last frozen movement came back to life, he simply shrugged his shoulders, turned on his heels, and made his way to his uncle's. He was, however, surprised to note that the 'tingle' he usually felt on rounding the corner before his house, did not happen until he reached the gate, and his uncle was not waiting for him on the top step. As he pressed the doorbell, Jimmy had a vaguely uneasy feeling, which certainly had never been there before. Also, he had to ring twice before the door opened; most un-Reuben-like.

"Hello Jim, old chap," Reuben started as usual. "How are you? Sorry I was a bit late opening the door; phone call don't you know. Kept me talking rather over long."

That certainly was *not* like Uncle Reuben. He didn't possess a telephone; rarely used them. Why would he then not tell him the truth? There was something not quite right. His initial doubts about whether it might not be his uncle were dispelled when he looked into those sharp, bright eyes. That it was Reuben was not in question. However, there was a sign around his eyes that not all was well. Since his return from Omni, he had learned to be wary and careful.

"Come in! Come in!" Reuben urged, as he ushered Jimmy quickly through the front door.

"Uncle?" Jimmy began, as he munched his way through his second piece of apple pie and ice cream.

"Yes, old chap, what is it you would like to know today?" Reuben returned, eyebrows raised.

"It's half question, half statement, really," Jimmy went on. "You know when you've been to Omni, and come

136

back? Well, you see, I've found that *things* have *changed* since I've been back. I wasn't able to concentrate in school for the first week or so, but at playtime yesterday, I 'thought' my way back ..."

"You *thought* your way back?" his uncle interrupted, quite surprised, or as surprised as Jimmy had ever seen him. "To Omni? How did you manage that?"

As Jimmy was now 'older' than when he had first visited Omni (well, a couple of months, at any rate) he felt able to shorten his version of events. However, when he reached the point at which he confronted Dwayne and Billy, and where everything stood still, Reuben silenced Jimmy with a gesture and ushered him into his study.

"Why have we come in here, uncle?" he asked, quite puzzled. He knew it must have *some* significance and importance, as a visit to Reuben's study was not an everyday occurrence. Reuben didn't offer to answer until the door was fast shut behind them.

The room hadn't changed at all save the desk top globe, which was no longer there. As Reuben opened his mouth to answer Jimmy's question, the room slid away from them, leaving them standing on a hillock amidst warring factions they did not recognise. They were there, but not there physically. All the smells and sights of the countryside invaded their nostrils and eyes, but they could not be seen other than by the Powers of the land. No sooner had they been, than they were back in the safety of the study. Reuben was obviously disturbed, but tried to hide it. Jimmy took it in his stride, and continued what he had been saying.

" And when I got back, I could focus much better on what was important," he went on. "I was top of my maths

137

class after break. Surprised my teacher, Mr Bolam."

"You must be very careful, my boy," Reuben continued, quietly and seriously, "not to allow anyone of this world to guess what might be happening in your life."

"I won't," he replied, "but why is it so important? No one else knows about Omni but us, do they?"

"It is important to make sure no one else does," Reuben replied, evading Jimmy's direct question. "There are still those who are watching and waiting for the right opportunity to attack."

This left Jimmy stunned. Uncle Reuben hadn't spoken like this before, either about Omni or about the possibilities of aggressive powers being anywhere other than in Omni. He had never seen Uncle Reuben anything other than jovial and good-humoured. 'Serious' and 'worried' were not words usually associated with him. Reuben, in fact, was rather concerned and quietly alarmed that Jimmy was developing the power to cross to Omni almost at will. This had never occurred before, not in all the years he had been associated with that world. Such power in one so young needed to be nurtured and protected, and to that end he would confer with the Powers for good in Omni. It needed a great deal of concentrated thought and will for even him to be able to use such power. If possessed by Seth or any other force for evil, all worlds linked to Omni would become ensnared and enslaved by evil.

"Uncle?" Jimmy went on after a moment or two's thought. "Could you explain why this Senti circlet has become so heavy and warm? In fact, it often glows in the dark."

"Circlet?" Reuben queried, a note of barely concealed

alarm entering his voice. "What circlet? Let me see it."

Jimmy delved deep into his coat inside pocket, and drew out the trophy he had brought back the first time he was there, and guarded carefully since then. By now, it was glowing only sullenly.

"Where did you get it?" he asked, urgently, catching his breath, "and how long have you had it? Does anyone else know of its existence? Truthfully now!"

Jimmy explained its history, at the end of which Reuben's shoulders dropped and he slumped into the big swivel chair behind the great oaken desk. "This is the worst news I have heard for many years and could prove our undoing."

"But it's only a ..." Jimmy butted in.

"You don't understand," Reuben interrupted again. "The circlet was not only a badge of office for the Senti you vanquished, it allows the power that made it to track its whereabouts. It could in part explain why you have had dreams and flashbacks since your return."

"In part?" Jimmy asked, puzzled.

"The other part is within you," Reuben said slowly. "Being in Omni over a prolonged period affects different people in different ways according to their inner power. Those with little inner strength or power are not affected. The stronger you are, the greater the effect. Ultimately, the ones with the greatest internal power learn to come and go between this world and Omni, and other worlds for that matter, at will. They are the people upon whom all our hopes are founded."

Jimmy sat in stunned silence throughout, recognising the importance of what his uncle was saying, and that the last bit referred to him. Yet, how could he, little ten-year-old Jimmy Scoggins, be this important person who held the future of *this* world, and, for that matter, others in his hands? Surely Uncle Reuben was mistaken in his assessment of Jimmy's capabilities. However, somehow, somewhere deep inside he knew he was right. He *did* feel different, strange.

"The circlet," Reuben said, jolting Jimmy back to reality, "you must not carry it again. Prolonged exposure to it will build into you dependence, and eventually it will turn your mind to the evil that made it. It must be destroyed, and the only person who can destroy it is you, I'm afraid, old man, in Omni itself."

"Destroy it? In Omni?" Jimmy exclaimed aghast. He hated the thought now of being without it, but Uncle Reuben was a wise old man. If he said so, it must be the only way. "But I don't know how or where in Omni."

"The Chieftain will know," answered Reuben, "and I will help you to get it to him, have no fear."

"Until then," Jimmy added, "can I keep it?"

"Only if you promise not to bring it out again," said Reuben. "You must not leave it anywhere, and don't touch it!"

As Reuben stopped talking, the great tapestry behind his desk began to descend slowly, silently. As they watched, a telecast of the battle they had witnessed first hand what seemed like moments before, began to roll. What was apparent to them was that it might have been an exact rerun of what they had witnessed, but *they* were not to be seen. Their little hillock was there, but they were not. Jimmy understood instantly, and started to explain to Reuben what he thought was happening. Reuben simply looked at him, in his own inimitable fashion, over his half-moon spectacles, not in any admonitory way, but with new wonder and respect in his eyes.

"You have grown indeed, old chap," he said slowly, choosing his words carefully. "The power of Old Omni is beginning to wax in you, and that is a sign for hope."

Jimmy listened carefully to what his uncle was saying, whilst watching the battle. "Look Uncle Reuben!" he burst in. "The battle's moved to Tarna's village!" At that moment, the telecast was lost, and the tapestry started to recoil.

"You must remember," Reuben added quietly, "that what you see is only *one* possible outcome. It *may* happen as you have seen it, but not necessarily."

Once again in the lounge, over a steaming cup of hot chocolate and piece of date and walnut cake, they watched the autumn light slip away over the back fence ahead of the blue dark of early evening.

"Time you were off, Old Chap," Reuben sighed. "Your mother will be nattering that you are late."

Jimmy's visit had given Reuben much to think about. He felt he had brought a new dimension to the fight against the evils of these worlds so much earlier than he had expected. He had always known there was something *different* about the lad, but he had not expected so much potential so soon.

Jimmy made his goodbyes and see-you-soons as he left the bottom-most step of his uncle's front path. He reached the gate on his way to catch his bus, and turned around to wave to his uncle, to see his own front door in front of him, and his hand on the latch of his own front gate.

Slightly puzzled, but not enormously surprised, he turned to tread the short way to his home. Even though he *thought* he had only just had hot chocolate and one of Reuben's enormous doorstep slabs of cake, his stomach felt curiously empty. That smell, as he unlatched the door, which assailed his nostrils was remarkably like cooking bacon and eggs, and *that* was designed to start his gastric juices flowing in anticipation. He had long stopped questioning how his mother was able to forecast at what time he would arrive for his tea, but that was mothers for you!

Tarna's village was beset by enemy forces. They fought against near impossible odds, but their defences held, just. Inside the Chieftain's hut the atmosphere was charged as in the build up to a catastrophic electrical storm. In the centre of the hut, in the deepening gloom, sat the Chieftain, eyes closed, hair cascading over his shoulders, hands grasping the deeply carved arms of the Great Chair. To the untrained observer, he was resting; to those who would know, he was engaged in an intense mental joust with some other, equally powerful being. Suddenly, he slumped forward, released from the contest, sweat coursing down his forehead. The gloom lifted, and the storm had passed, for now. The defenders had repulsed the enemy, but he knew that this was only the beginning of a much more intense onslaught which would follow in its wake.

The Chieftain's eyes drew slowly open, and *then* he knew they had been betrayed.

142

Chapter Sixteen

Jimmy had yet another fitful night, with vivid dreams of Omni invading his subconscious. So vivid were they that he could feel the sun on the top of his head and experience those smells that were particular only to that world. For the most part, his presence there was disjointed and illogical, but it also wound a thread of truth, a reality which could not be doubted. Mostly, he re-enacted and revisited previous experiences and places, but generally out of sync with everything else.

He saw their approach to Algan's cave, but he was the one who was injured at the threshold. Dwayne Davis, who was substituted for his brother, was looking down at him as he came to. Within moments, he awoke in Oompah's castle, where Dominic was the toad and Oompah turned into Grumblin' Grainger. This in turn gave way to the Chieftain's hut, but the Chieftain was not in his Great Chair, or at least he didn't recognise him as such from behind. The gloom and mist surrounding the chair and its occupant masked his upper body and head, until the room revolved around the chair, and revealed – Tarna! Tarna? What was he doing there? And to whom was he talking?

"It shall be done master," Tarna muttered, but seemed unable to move whilst visibly struggling to disengage from the conversation.

Jimmy seemed held, enthralled by what he had seen and heard. The over-riding questions in his mind were – why was he in the Chieftain's chair, and at who was the comment directed? Only the Chieftain of All Omni was permitted to sit in *that* chair. Was he talking to the Chieftain? No, it couldn't have been, as he would not have allowed him to be there. Was this a presage of the future, with Tarna as Chieftain? But the lineage of that position was unbroken father to son, and the Chieftain had five sons.

Jimmy dismissed it as part of the nonsense of a dream, until he heard Tarna's last words.

"Yes, my lord Seth, I obey," Tarna croaked whilst bowing his head.

The visions of Omni slowly faded and drifted away, leaving Jimmy once again restlessly tossing and turning in his bed. The light of dawn was beginning to sneak through the chink in his curtains, as he started to resurface. He awoke with a start to the milkman's crate rattling on their top step. Eyes blearily open, the night left him with only one enduring impression; Tarna, a traitor?

School was almost a relief after the disturbing dreams of the night before. He had tried to share his experiences with his brother, but Tommy had no longer any interest in Omni, and so refused to listen or talk about it. His mind was firmly on other, more important, things like his friends, football, and girls. Jimmy and he were no longer co-adventurers in a dangerous and exciting world.

"Grow up Jimmy. This place 'Omni' lives only in your imagination," was Tommy's parting comment, making

Jimmy believe that Tommy was in some sort of denial. How could he feel like that, after all they had been through together?

The first faces he encountered on entering the playground at a quarter to nine were, of course, Dwayne and Billy, their sullenness casting a shadow in their 'skulking corner', as Mr Bolam called it. He was aware, was Mr Bolam, of what they were like but hadn't had any complaints from other children to allow him to do something about them. That had begun to change, Jimmy had seen to that. As soon as he saw them, he began to 'feel' their animosity towards him. It was a similar feeling to those he had experienced, when he and Tommy were overwhelmed by the Senti in Seth's castle, and when they had almost become stuck in the Foggy Land of Four.

He had had these feelings around Dwayne for a little while, only now were they beginning to become clearer. Although Dwayne was wary about Jimmy, his thoughts betrayed his inner feelings; thoughts that Jimmy could read and understand! Don't ask how he could do it, he just could, and he was even more surprised when he realised that Dwayne's thoughts would suddenly stop when Jimmy anticipated them. He had somehow stumbled on the way to intercept thoughts from other people. He couldn't do it for every thought; just the aggressive ones came through to him. He had developed the ability to redirect or change or interrupt or divert them, making the 'thinker' lose track of what he was thinking.

"Hello," came a small voice just behind. He turned sharply to see a raven-haired girl, dressed in a black skirt and bright red cardigan. She was smaller than Jimmy, who had grown somewhat since the summer; all that good food, according to his mum. Her eyes caught his, and dropped him into deep inner pools he had experienced only when he had been in Omni. He had neither seen nor met her before, certainly not here; or had he? He stared at her, trying to place her.

"It's rude to stare and not speak. My dad always says so," she interrupted his thoughts.

"I'm sorry," he excused himself, "but I don't think we've met before. Are you new? I'm Jimmy."

"No," she returned deliberately. "I've been here a long time. It's just that you've never noticed me before. I'm Ursula." There was something about Ursula that struck a chord within Jimmy, so that he knew instantly they were going to become friends. Along with many other things, Jimmy seemed to have developed a very sharp instinct when it came to people.

"I like you," Jimmy said, rather disarmingly. "Can we be friends?"

"I think so," Ursula replied, seeming to give it an age of thought and consideration, but within that split second, they both knew that their embryo friendship was cemented. They had been, and would be friends forever.

"Are you sure you've been here for a long time?" Jimmy asked simply as they filed into class once the bell had sounded. "It's just that I'm sure I would have noticed you….I think."

Ursula smiled and inclined her head slightly. "Yes," she thought, "I am going to enjoy being with you."

She was the sort of person who could easily be missed in an otherwise busy school. She was small and almost invisible because she didn't put herself out to be noticed.

146

It's not that she lacked confidence because of some learning difficulty – she was incredibly bright with an innate ability to adapt quickly to different learning environments – she just didn't see the need to be 'noticed' for the sake of it.

Still unsure of the veracity of Ursula's insistence that she had always been part of his class, Jimmy settled in his desk to his morning's work. Despite giving a much more successful impression that he was concentrating closely on his work history was not where his heart lay. The love life of Henry VIII and the lives of the Tudors in general just didn't do it for Jimmy. All that waste of …

"Just you wait, Jimmy Scoggins," he felt in his mind. "I'll catch you when you are least expecting it, and …" Dwayne Davis just didn't understand how uncomfortable his life was about to become by popping into Jimmy's mind in that quasi-kamikaze fashion. Jimmy turned his mind towards the intrusion, and his face towards Dwayne, just in time to see him wince and recoil physically as if warding off a blow, and to hear him screech loudly in pain. Jimmy knew it wasn't him because he had only just caught Dwayne's intent. Then who? What? He noticed a slight movement from the corner of his eye, over by the filing cabinet at the back of the room. Ursula? A slight, almost imperceptible smile played at the edges of her lips, and as Jimmy turned back to his books and the lesson, he was convinced Ursula wasn't of this class, or of *this* world either, for that matter.

Dwayne continued to hold the sides of his head, whilst whimpering pitifully, until Mr Bolam snapped at him, "For goodness sake, Dwayne Davis, either stop being so soft or go home. I'm sure no-one will think any less of you if you do." The sarcasm lay heavily on the last sentence.

There were several sniggers from the back of the room, which, of course, made his decision for him. He spent the rest of the day sulking silently, as far from the others as he was able to get.

Jimmy couldn't wait for lunchtime to talk to Ursula about what had happened, but she wasn't to be found anywhere. He hadn't seen her leave, and he was sure she didn't have an appointment anywhere. Where had she gone, and, more urgently, where had she come from in the first place? He thought he might have the answer to that one, but he needed to confront her with his suspicions.

At the end of the school day, he hung around the yard for a little while, hoping to catch her on her way home, but to no avail. It was only when he heard the familiar almost inaudible "Hello" that he spun on his heels, to find her behind him.

"Ursula!" he blurted out. "Where've you been this afternoon? I missed you at lunch. Did you have an appointment? I wanted to talk to you."

"No appointment," she replied matter-of-factly. "I've been in school all day."

Jimmy stopped abruptly, a puzzled frown growing on his face as he stared into her eyes, not quite believing what he was hearing.

"Now hang on a bit!" he burst in. "I'm not *that* stupid. You were supposed to be in art this afternoon, and I didn't see you there."

"Peripatetic violin," she replied softly.

"OK," he went on, "I'll give you that, but the last half hour was story, and you weren't there." At first he was quite anxious to find out where she had been, but found his mind becoming less and less perturbed the more he spoke, until he found what he had wanted to know was no longer urgent.

They walked along in silence for a few moments until they reached her house. Once they had stopped outside her gate, Jimmy realised that either he had never been past this house on his way to or from school before, or he had taken a wrong turning in his eagerness to be with Ursula. Had she somehow taken him out of his way without his noticing it? *This* house was definitely not on *his* street, and he had never seen such countryside out of Omni.

The house and grounds were set apart from the other dwellings hereabouts by an enormous palisade fence which was hugely overgrown by a vast yew hedge; the sort that must have been there for the last hundred years or more. Breached by none except the smallest of animals, it gave the impression of mystery and invulnerability. The gates grew out of the yew and were purely and simply solid oak, constructed in the same style as his Uncle Reuben's fence; allowing that comfortable impenetrability for someone who needed security and seclusion. "Who would wish such a degree of invisibility?" Jimmy pondered.

As for the house itself, over the gate Jimmy could see only the upper floor, with its crenellated and turreted roof, and part of the gable end which was covered by autumnally coloured Virginia Creeper. Dour grey granite blocks, rather reminiscent of ancient Scottish castles, spattered with bilious green lichenous patches anchored this edifice to the bones of the earth. Unimaginably large and old, from where Jimmy stood, it brought back half-hidden memories of his incarceration in Seth's castle, vividly and uncomfortably to his unfortunately overactive consciousness. *That* was something he didn't need to remember, thank you very much.

"This is where I live," Ursula said, looking into Jimmy's still incredulous eyes. "I know we made a slight detour, but I'm glad you came with me."

"Slight!?" he thought. "This is the biggest 'slight' *I've* ever experienced!"

"Something I need to ask you before I go," Jimmy proffered tentatively. "It *was* you wasn't it when Dwayne began to express his thoughts about me in class?"

"I'm sure I don't know what you mean," she replied demurely, a slight smile hovering around the corners of her mouth.

Jimmy knew immediately that he need ask no further and that the subject was now closed. This, of course, served to draw him closer to her in shared experience and purpose.

"Would you like to come and stay the weekend and meet my dad?" Ursula asked.

"Certainly would!" he blurted out. "I'm sure my mum would be fine with that, if your dad would be."

Jimmy's mum's approval was a source of excitement for him, not only because he was allowed to stay the weekend at Ursula's, but also because it gave him an excuse to make an unscheduled visit to his Uncle Reuben's to share with him his new friend. Perhaps he might help with understanding her, and where she came from. He had his suspicions, of course, but he felt he would like some sort of confirmation from him.

As it was early autumn, the nights were still light until quite late, and would be so until the clocks went back in late October. Consequently, he would be able to visit Uncle Reuben's by bus and return before dark. The buses remained quite frequent because the winter timetable with its restricted service was still weeks away. Home for four, tea by quarter to five, catch the quarter past five bus, was his goal so that he would be at his uncle's house by a quarter to six. He would then be able to catch the twenty-five past seven bus home so he would be back by eightish, in time for supper and bed. There was another bus back at twenty-five to eight but that took forever because it detoured to another depot to pick up bus company workers on their way home.

The first parts of his plan successfully executed, his bus ride was uneventful if a little nerve-racking, mostly because of what had happened on his last visit. This time he didn't quite know what to expect, although he *hoped* things might have returned to how they were that day he made his first visit to Omni; 'Parcel Day' as he often referred to it since. He reached Tumbles Row more quickly than he had anticipated; no more inter-galactic adventures, just concerned thought about the issues which were bothering him and about which he desperately needed Reuben's counsel. This was the part of the journey he loved the most; that tingle of anticipation and excitement at seeing his uncle's back fence around the next corner and then Reuben standing on the top step at the front of his house. Only, the expected 'tingle' was not there, and neither was the fence as he rounded the corner.

That had been replaced by a hugely unruly privet hedge which hadn't seen shears for many months, and seemingly impenetrable from root to crown. Jimmy stopped, and looked around, scratching his head, profoundly puzzled. This *was* the right street and it *was* Uncle Reuben's house, he was sure. He was used to the garden being different every time he visited, but that was inside. The outer fence boundary had always been the same. He rounded the front of the house, to be stopped in his tracks as if hit by a cricket bat.

In the front garden by the lilac tree in the corner there grew, as if it had been there forever, a large dirty white sign, which deflated him and rocked him back on his heels.

He couldn't believe that his Uncle Reuben's house, that wonderful exciting place which had thrown up so many unexpected things, was now for sale! There was no sign of life. The curtains were closed and there was no smoke coming from the chimney, a sure sign that Reuben was not at home.

Chapter Seventeen

"I've already told you, mum," Jimmy insisted, "that it *was* Uncle Reuben's house, *he* wasn't there, and the house *was* for sale. All you have to do is phone him and then phone the agent."

"You know as well as I do that he doesn't hold with telephones," she returned, "and so doesn't have one."

"He does now," Jimmy returned quickly. "*He* phoned *me* not long ago, remember? If you don't believe me look back in your phone records."

"Oh, I don't know," she sighed with a resigned shrug of the shoulders. "I've got too much to do to be proving and finding out. I'm sure he will get in touch when he's good and ready. He always did spend a lot of time travelling. I was always given to understand it was a lot to do with his businesses."

Jimmy sank back into the big easy chair by the front window, his mind trying to come to terms with the mysterious disappearance of his uncle. It was a good job he was spending time at Ursula's house this coming weekend. Perhaps she might be able to shed some light on this new turn of events. He was looking forward to having someone to talk to, someone to share his thoughts with, about his many concerns. He *would* raise the issue of Omni at some stage with her although he felt he already knew what her response would be. There was only the obstacle of three days' schooling getting in the way. School! Was he going to have trouble with Dwayne again? He didn't think so, but if he did, he thought he would know what to do. How many ways could there be to 'encourage' him and his soft sidekick to back off?

It was a worrying week for Jimmy. School wasn't the problem as he could look after himself, at last, as far as the former bully Dwayne Davis was concerned, and, of course others like him. Classes had become easy to negotiate particularly if you applied the well-tried formula – do all that is expected of you, don't cause any problems, and, above all, remain invisible! He was learning fast which made it easier for him to adapt to any situation that might occur. He might now take most things in his stride, but what was having a profound effect on him was the not knowing what had happened to Reuben.

Inevitably, despite his concerns and apprehensions, Friday arrived. School was no big deal, as they never did much anyway on Fridays, but the excitement of the weekend in prospect was beginning to kick in. What did he expect to achieve by spending the time with Ursula and her parents, and what was he expecting to find in that enormous old house?

"Have you packed clean underwear?" Jimmy's mother asked. "And what about a clean shirt?"

"Mother!" Jimmy sighed. "I'm only staying until Sunday. It's not an expedition to the other side of the world!" Those words kind of rang in his head because he never knew *where* he might end up. In fact, he rather hoped something good *was* going to happen.

"Well, hurry up dear," she went on matter-of-factly. "Your taxi will be here shortly."

"Taxi?" Jimmy shouted, not quite believing his ears. "It's only a short distance away. I can walk it in no time…"

"And get dirty and sweaty into the bargain!" she interrupted rather sharply. "If you're spending time in someone else's home, under some one else's sheets, you *will* be clean when you get there." And that was the end of the conversation. He knew when *not* to answer back, and this was one of those times.

The taxi was on time and it dropped him outside Ursula's front gate. Bit of a misnomer really, he thought. More like a portcullis than a gate. He was half-expecting a moat and drawbridge to appear. There was, however, a rather large iron bell-pull handle by the gate, which he felt he ought to grasp, as he didn't want to spend his evening on the pavement. It was actually more akin to a compacted mud path than a pavement, with tufts of grass growing through in places, telling him that the path wasn't well-trodden. He hesitated, touched the bell-pull but shied away before making solid contact with the cold metal. This he did several times until he took courage and yanked the metal downwards with an almighty jerk. It hung loosely by the gate and, as nothing happened, he assumed rather worriedly that he had broken it. However, it did return slowly to its original starting point, but still nothing happened. Five minutes elapsed when a faint whirring sound drew his attention to the slight inward movement of the great gates. They opened, only enough to allow one smallish person to pass through with a squeeze, and suddenly he was in. The gates shut fast once again behind him. He wasn't at all prepared for what he saw within the grounds.

As far as the eye could see, there were grounds of lawn, shrub, and wild grassland. It was reminiscent of his Uncle Reuben's garden, but much grander in scale, with many more trees and a wider variety of hiding and exploration places. He had visited his uncle's house and explored his garden more times than he could remember but even that couldn't compare with the vista now before him. Every time he had been to his uncle's there had been something different to do, somewhere different to explore, but here it was as if *all* those areas had been joined together in one place. The driveway, which could accommodate five or six normal-sized cars, was entirely black-topped. The surrounding paths leading to and from the house were paved with small riven slabs, which had a vaguely worn yellow cast that reflected the hue of the golden pea gravel surrounding them.

The house was altogether something else. It was larger than anything he had ever seen, both in this world and in Omni – save Oompah's and Seth's castles, although he had only ever really seen the *inside* of Seth's castle. Standing at the front of it, as he had come in through the gate, he couldn't see an end to it. He could have been forgiven for believing there was nothing else to this view but house! A mixture of styles and materials, it seemed not to be from any one particular era. Part gothic, part Tudor, part Victorian; it wasn't at all clear when the main foundation to the building had been laid. He could have had an enormous amount of fun exploring both house and grounds, if he had a *year* free to do it justice. He turned purposefully on his heels to head for the front entrance which was blocked by a giant double door, probably cut from an oak tree centuries in the growing, to see the diminutive form of Ursula watching him from the cover of the portico which sheltered the entrance.

"Hello," she said with little outward emotion. "I'm glad you could come. Please enter." Whereupon, she turned and disappeared into the gloomy interior, that from where Jimmy was standing, matched the exterior of the building.

The hallway which smelt of still air and baking, must have been big enough to house his own home in its entirety very comfortably. There were four polished oaken doors off to the left and two to the right, hiding goodness knows what treasures to explore. The central staircase raised its magnificently brass-clad oak treads to the heavens, splitting into two galleried landings that shot off in opposite directions at the first floor. The great sweeping curved banisters, which again were fashioned from enormous pieces of wood, ended with flattened and curled newel posts. They would have been ideal for sliding had it not been for five giant, but highly polished, brass studs set at four feet intervals along their lengths, making sliding somewhat hazardous. Jimmy simply stood in the middle of that cavernous room, his mouth ever-so-slightly agape.

"Wow!" Jimmy said at last. "I know this will sound silly, but is this *really your* house?"

"Yes," Ursula puzzled, brow frowning slightly. "We've been here for as long as I can remember."

"Will I get to meet your dad as well as your mum?" he

asked.

"My dad, yes. Mum's dead," she replied quite matter-of-fact.

"Oh, I'm ever so sorry. I …" he tailed off, a little embarrassed at what he thought to be a huge blunder.

"Don't be," she replied. "She died when I was very young and so I don't really remember much about her. Mum and dad bought this house before I was born so it's been in the family over twenty years. Dad will be in later, much later usually, because he's a scientist; works for the government or something. Come on. I'll show you to your room."

The central staircase was magnificent; almost as long, grand and sweeping as the sumptuously carpeted and brass-rodded walk way in one of those grand country houses of the 18th century; although definitely not as busy or noisy. The walls on the landings were covered with exquisitely executed paintings, which seemed mainly to be of random countryside, depicting very busy scenes of agricultural activities or battles or fabulous animal interactions. Obviously through a trick of the light the scenes were so cleverly painted that they gave the distinct impression of movement. He particularly liked the one near to his room showing a group of people toiling through a cooling forest on a hot day. The movement was so real, the dappled shade of the forest so soothing and the smell of resinous wood so pungent in his nostrils, that he could have been in …

"Your bedroom will, I am sure, be very comfortable," Ursula interrupted his reverie. "If you need anything just ask. There is a bell by the bed to summon Etherington, dad's butler. Please be aware that if you were to wander without me, you would most likely become lost. Mrs Tuliver, the cook, will have something ready for us to eat in half an hour or so. I'll come back for you then." And with that she was away to her own room.

His bedroom was a surprise. He was expecting some old fashioned place with a four-poster bed and tapestries on the walls, and in that respect he was disappointed. The room was incredibly large by the standard of his own home. There *were* lots of period features – huge sash windows, picture rail, and deep carved skirting boards and doorframes – but essentially it was decorated in a modern style, with an ordinary divan bed and bedroom furniture. What *did* catch his eye were the half-dozen or so very large paintings hanging randomly around the walls, which seemed to him to be a continuation of each other, and which, if hung end to end, would have made a large continuously active mural. There was a new folded bathrobe on his bed, which he didn't know what to do with, and a set of thick towels, which he did. The dark-stained oak floorboards were only partially covered by a huge tapestry-style rug, which seemed to have been woven with much the same sort of pictures as the paintings. So here he was, in a hall of a bedroom, which gave the impression of being in the midst of a wonderfully active and multi-faceted countryside.

"Shall we explore a bit?" Ursula rounded on Jimmy once tea had been eaten and was on the way to being forgotten. She knew instinctively that he would agree readily and so it was really a tease on her part. They decided to do all the rooms downstairs first, which should have been relatively quick and easy, but once in the drawing room it was obvious to Ursula that it would take much longer than she had anticipated; Jimmy just had to examine everything hanging on the walls.

Through the drawing room and into the mirrored gallery Jimmy paused in front of a painting. It was a close-up of part of an ancient building, which resembled castles he had seen before. In the distance could be seen lines of cavalry, decked in their splendid armour, carrying multi-coloured pennants and banners which streamed out behind as they cantered into a brisk breeze. Jimmy watched in awe as the breeze touched his face and he felt the brazen hooves thundering the hard earth. He cast a glance sideways towards Ursula to see if she could see what he saw, feel what he felt. But where she had been standing, close to his shoulder, was the knotty bole of some un-guessable high tree with many others beyond. He was beneath the outwardly eaves of a forest he recognised and which he had visited many times before. The flash of sun on a highly polished shield blinded him temporarily and, the instant he unscrewed his eyes, he caught the intent and intense gaze of his companion. He was in the mirror gallery once again.

"You were there, weren't you?" she asked immediately, giving him no time to collect his senses.

"Yes ... No! I'm sure I don't know what you mean," Jimmy stammered, taken very much off guard. Although he had a 'feeling' about Ursula and shared a certain bond he had never shared with anyone before, not even Tommy, there was still something mysterious about her.

"Oh yes you do! You know," she demanded, "that other world; the place where you got that ... that circlet thing you keep in your pocket."

That revelation staggered him so much that he had to sit down on one of the Chaises Longue close by.

"How did you know?" was all he could say, lamely. Although he wasn't about to give anything away to any Tom, Dick or Harriet, it was obvious to him she *was* special, and it would be safe to share certain things with her.

"It is called Omni," he started, "you know, the place I've been to?"

They moved quietly back to the drawing room to be more comfortable in the great, deep leather armchairs by the chimney breast fireplace. Its grate by now was glowing fiercely from a log fire which had been set in their absence. Although he missed out no important factor, he gave her a much edited and slicker version of his Omni adventures; otherwise they would still have been there a week later. Even so, late afternoon changed to mid-evening before he had finished his story. Throughout she remained silent, neither interrupting nor asking the sort of questions most other youngsters would have thrown at him. It was almost as if she knew and was simply awaiting his confirmation of her intuition.

"You were right," he finished. "I *was* there when we were in the mirror room. These paintings on the walls, I think, are all of some aspect of Omni, and what is more they are all active, alive, moving, albeit very slowly. I spent what seemed like an age under the eaves of a forest I have been to before, many times; the Shifting Forest of Linden. I saw gathering companies of horsemen in their war armour, mounted on huge black horses, moving to battle. I seemed to be there from late afternoon to that

161

twilight time which ushers in the velvety black dark of night."

"But," she stammered, incredulous at what she had heard, "you were gone only long enough for me to notice; only seconds, the mere blinking of an eye. How is that possible?"

During the time he had been recounting his story, they had moved slowly along a wide, thickly carpeted passageway whose walls were festooned with rich tapestries. This had the effect of deadening everything they had to say; where words hit the walls and were absorbed by the tapestries. Suddenly, passing what seemed to be a dark doorway, which was recessed quite deeply into the thick walls, Jimmy experienced a distinct tingling sensation throughout his body; a tingling he *had* felt many times before. He stopped in front of the doorway, his hand lightly resting on Ursula's forearm, signalling her to stop. He noticed a door in the depths of the recess's gloom, which was fashioned from thick oaken staves, stained dark and giving off a slight sheen. The most surprising thing about it, however, was that no handle or knob could be seen.

"What's behind that door?" Jimmy croaked, almost inaudibly.

"Why?" she asked in return.

"It's important," he hissed. "Just tell me and I'll explain later."

"My father's study," she answered, not knowing why it was so important but noticing the startling effect this information had on her companion.

Yes, it was Omni Jimmy had found himself in, fleetingly in his real time, but several hours Omni time. The horsemen, he had never seen before, but they were very real and *were* preparing for war, although Jimmy did not know whether they were for good or ill. In his previous time in Omni, whilst there were periods when there was slight concern over the outcome of his actions, there was never any *real* doubt as to whether he would survive. He had had that much confidence in his guardians. Now, however, was an entirely different matter. The situation he found himself in was much more serious, and seemed to be running away from him, being no longer a game. The stakes were much higher and the outcome was now, for the first time, in doubt.

"Why were you so concerned about my father's study?" Ursula asked, once they had reached the lounge at the back of the house. Of giant proportions and fully carpeted, this room was different from all the others he had seen. Although magnificently furnished and decorated two major points struck him immediately they sat down. There was no oak in the room at all, and the walls were entirely bare of pictures and paintings. For some reason, the room was airier, lighter and less oppressive than elsewhere in the house. Even though dusk was creeping in, the huge conservatory seemed to generate light, probably because it was west-facing and the last vestiges of sun always lingered longest at this side of the house.

"Two reasons really; whenever I visited my Uncle Reuben's," he explained, "I always felt a tingling sensation as I approached his house. It's how I *knew* I was there, as most of the houses in the streets around were almost identical. Secondly, the door not only bore a striking resemblance to *his* study door, it also shared the same lack of a handle. I know this one *is* used regularly because the floor carpet to it is well-worn, so there must be some way in. Another thing; when I visited my uncle the other day, there was *no* tingle, and his house was empty; it was for sale."

"Are you suggesting that *my* father is in some way tied up with the disappearance of *your* uncle?" Ursula asked rather sharply. "My father, I'll have you know, is a respected scientist so he can't be involved!"

"I wasn't suggesting for a moment he was!" Jimmy replied defensively. "I was simply suggesting that there were certain similarities. If your father could help me to track down my Uncle Reuben I should be mightily grateful."

A great rolling boom split the night, splashing intense blue light across the Southern Standing Stones. In the after-flash the tall figure of a black rider was visible standing in the stirrups of an equally black steed. The Faceless Horseman only appeared at times of greatest need, and matters seemed to be moving inexorably towards an unthinkable conclusion. The Stones lit up again to reveal a change in the rider's position. Still standing in the stirrups, horse unmoving save the occasional flick of the tail and snorting of the nostrils, he remained upright, every sinew stretched and taut, straining to catch the subtle changes he had recognised in the vapours above him. He turned deliberately, the back of his head swivelling slowly side to side, as if sensing the air to detect any unusual activity; any developing threat. Without warning his face was revealed; that empty and featureless visage, seen during his last visit to this on-going conflict, now had eyes of an incalculable depth and sharpness! Those eyes could see what his mind had long since known. Now, he was more than ready for the test.

Chapter Eighteen

"Why are there no family photographs in your house?" Jimmy asked at Saturday lunch, his mouth full of Victoria sponge.

"Why do you ask?" she replied, rather puzzled at his strange interest.

"Well," he explained, "most people I have visited have at least one photo of either some*one* in their house, or a family group shot. My mum says … "

"Mum and dad were always too busy with the *important* things of life to waste time having photos taken," she broke in sharply. "They always said that thoughts and memories were much more important and lasted much longer than an image on a piece of shiny paper."

"I know your dad's a scientist," Jimmy stated matter-of-factly, "and a very important one I am sure," he added hurriedly, realising that his first statement sounded condescendingly abrupt, drawing a slight smile from Ursula. Jimmy hoped it didn't seem that he was trying too hard not to offend, which Ursula obviously appreciated. "But what did your mum do, apart from being a mum, of course. What was she called?"

Ursula pondered for a few moments, a slightly wistful look clouding her face, before she replied. "She was very beautiful, with dark brown hair and deep eyes; that much I recollect vividly. I don't really know what she did, but I think it involved a lot of travelling to other … places. She was called Miriel."

Miriel! Did she say Miriel? Jimmy dropped his cake fork with an almighty clatter. He felt his lower lip slowly fall open, making him look silly and feel like he had publicly made a huge fool of himself. He tried to utter the name, but couldn't even approximate its sound. Was Miriel the young girl in Seth's castle who helped him to escape? Was she the reason why he was now here? Was she really the same person, a sorcerer's daughter and another's niece, who is the mother of the friend now sitting before him? This could not be!

"I once knew a girl," Jimmy started slowly, after several minutes of thoughtful silence, "who was the daughter of a powerful sorcerer for good, and also the niece of another powerful sorcerer but for evil. She has a special place in my heart because it was she who saved my life by helping our Tommy and me to escape the clutches of her uncle the evil Lord of Seth, otherwise known as Tar-igor. Her father, Gor-ifan, had been defeated by his brother and his body supposedly buried in the mountains. *That* girl's name was Miriel."

At this Ursula's countenance gradually drained of colour, to take on that ashen hue of someone who is about to pass out. Hearing Jimmy's description, and the story of his escape, those names resurrected a recognition deep within her subconscious.

"I am convinced that the Miriel who saved you *was* my mother," said Ursula shakily.

"But that's impossible!" Jimmy blurted out. "She was only my age when I was in Omni for the first time, and that's only about three months ago in … our time." His last words dropped out of real time and slowed to a complete halt half way through "time". The ending of the word he simply mouthed soundlessly. He had remembered, of course, that 'real' time is much slower than Omni time, and so a lifetime could have passed in the few months he had been back in his world. That would explain to some extent the apparent advanced age of Tarna.

"Who then is your father? Is he someone I've already met in Omni or is he really a scientist?" Jimmy asked seriously, *knowing* her ancestry but not actually knowing anything *about* them. "I know your grandfather, or at least I've met him fleetingly. He was the Old Man of the Mountains, and a very frightening man, I can tell you!"

"I've never met him," Ursula replied, "but we have an early portrait of him in the Great Hall."

"Wow!" was all that Jimmy could say, quite overwhelmed by this little snippet of news. At times, Ursula seemed to talk in snippets; little pieces of what seemed to be innocuous information but which were quite important. "Can we see it?"

"Of course," she replied. "Come on." She was out of her seat and away down the passageway before he had stood up. He had to move quickly so that he didn't lose her. Now, *this* passageway seemed familiar, and should, he thought, have led to her father's study. But no; the carpet was different and showed hardly any signs of wear, which meant the corridor had been little used. The walls were bare of all hangings, whether portraits or tapestries, and there were no hidden doorways. The passageway seemed to bend and curve first one way then another and Jimmy had great difficulty keeping up with his companion, let alone catching her. Very briefly he caught a glimpse of her back disappearing around the next-corner-but-one as he reached each in turn. Suddenly, rounding a blind corner, he exploded into an enormous Great Hall, as a cork would explode from a bottle of shaken fizzy wine, his momentum had been so great. Had he not smacked his shins on a large footstool blocking his way and then catapulted into an enormously deep and soft settee, his headlong trajectory would have taken him through one of the huge arched windows, which filled one wall of the room.

Inside the room he saw a high ceiling, with a great expanse of painted walls and relief moulding, depicting images of what could only be described as generally 'Omni' country life. One wall of the room was made up entirely of arched windows, each of which was perhaps two to three times his height, essentially making a wall of glass. This looked out onto the rolling countryside which was not countryside at all, but the extensive grounds in which the house was set. The outer end of the room allowed passage to a formal rose garden through a spectacular set of rose wood French doors. Jimmy found Ursula waiting for him at the end of a very long wall, which was dressed with row upon row of portraits.

"Wow!" Jimmy gasped. "Is this all *your* ancestry?"

"I don't know," Ursula replied. "I *think* so. I know that lots of these" − and here she swept her arm across the whole wall − "are ancestors, but how many, I'm not rightly sure." She paused for a brief moment, head lowered, brows furrowed, deep in thought, and then continued moving quickly to the middle of the wall. "*This* is my grandfather, whose name I didn't know until you

169

told it to me earlier. I knew him only as Gangan."

The face was a little less hairy than the last time he had seen him, but there could be no doubt that this was the Old Man of the Mountains, Gor-ifan, Ursula's grandfather. As soon as Jimmy saw the eyes he was transfixed, in the same way his attention had been held when he and Tommy had met the old sorcerer before. It was almost as if the picture was trying to probe his mind, but that wasn't possible. A picture was simply paint, with no life of its own; only, Jimmy wasn't so sure. His attention was finally drawn away from the picture only when Ursula interrupted his thoughts.

"Is this how you remember him?" she said.

"More or less," he replied, dragging his eyes across to meet her gaze, "give or take a little of the facial hair." His eyes drifted back slowly, as if trying to sneak a look when he had been told not to. "He's moved!" he blurted out. "The picture's not the same!"

"That's not possible!" Ursula returned. "Pictures are not alive. They can't just … move."

"I'm telling you it has!" he argued, almost hopping from foot to foot. "If you remember, his was a full-face portrait. It's how I recognised him because it's how I saw him last. Now the picture is in profile, you know, side view. Look!"

She followed his pointing finger and realised at once that he was right. The portrait had changed its position and now a power had begun to wax in the picture, drawing them to it so that they were almost touching its surface with their noses. They strained to resist, eyelids screwed shut in an effort not to make contact with the canvas. Unexpectedly, they were released and as they opened their eyes slowly as if waking after a long sleep, they felt the caressing warmth of a welcoming sun on their faces. They were in the southern hills of Omni confronted by a grizzled old man with sharp, deep eyes.

"So we meet at last," he growled in a deep guttural drawl. It was Gor-ifan, the Old Man of the Mountains, Ursula's grandfather.

"Grandfather," Ursula whispered, quite overcome with emotion, although it didn't sit well with her. "I never thought… "Her voice tailed off, as tears began to well in her eyes.

"My child," he growled softly, reaching out to her with one old and gnarled hand. Such touches of tenderness towards another had been alien to him over recent years, particularly since his brother had been largely instrumental in his demise. Perhaps now that he was regaining his powers, slowly, painstakingly, surreptitiously, he might once again retake his rightful place in what had become an alien world to him.

Although at this moment Ursula felt nothing for this world, her inner feelings told her she had always known this man, as if he had always been part of her. Deep inside stirred a desire for, and to know more about, the world she had never visited until now. It fused through her very bones, the countless generations of contact, line on line, to her, the latest, and possibly the last. She was not about to lose her grandfather now and she was prepared to do whatever it might take to stay here with him. Unfortunately, as Jimmy had found before, Omni travel could neither be guaranteed nor relied upon. When it was your time to return *that* world would find a way to bring you back. The same was true in reverse, as she

171

discovered. With one blink she stood in front of her grandfather, holding his great hairy hand tightly, and the next they were in the grounds of her home, standing with her nose to a knotty oak tree and grasping Jimmy's hand as tightly as she could.

"Hand please Ursula," Jimmy said quietly.

"What?" she replied, still really in Omni. "What do you mean?"

"Your finger nails are nearly through my almost dead hand!" he grimaced in pain, trying to draw his hand away from hers.

"Can we not go back?" she said to him, earnestly gazing into his eyes. "You know, like straight away, now?"

"I'm afraid it doesn't quite work like that," he told her quite authoritatively, speaking from experience. "Omni travel is not a bus service where you can hop on whenever you have a mind. *It* decides when it wants to take *you*, and usually there is some purpose to it. It's not just a day out, you know."

"I know," she nodded quite wistfully, "but that's the first time I've seen my grandfather, and now he's gone." She turned to Jimmy, eyes pleading whilst tears rolled down her cheeks, and automatically he slipped his arm around her heaving shoulders, in an attempt to comfort her.

That night Jimmy slept the most soundly he had slept for many weeks and so he awoke and arose refreshed and revitalised. Although breakfast was a bright affair it wasn't matched by the weather. Chill, dull and drizzly, it seemed to have left the last vestiges of summer behind and was rushing headlong into an early winter. Ursula was late for breakfast and sat down in front of Jimmy, her eyes betraying her lack of sleep. She seemed distracted and distant, no doubt feeling keenly the loss of her grandfather so soon after finding him for the first time.

"That's the only time I've been there," she said finally. "I've always *felt* there was somewhere, another place, because of being around my mother. *That* I know now. I always knew I was *different* from everyone else because I never "fitted" in wherever I was. When do you think we might return?"

"You never can tell, really," he replied quietly, sensing the sensitivity of the moment and her impatience. "Once you've been, Omni can call you back any time it needs you, as I told you yesterday. It was yesterday, wasn't it? Seems like forever ago. Let's go for a wander down the corridor by your father's study, you know, where we felt the tingle. You never know, you might get lucky."

Ursula agreed, almost reluctantly, and led the way. They took the exact turning they needed, followed the corridor to where her father's study should have been, but couldn't find it. How could it be possible to lose a whole corridor and a study when there was only one possible way? When they emerged into the hall through one of the oaken doorways they had not used before, they both slowed to a frustrated halt, looked at each other and shrugged in disbelief.

"I don't believe this!" Jimmy sighed. "How could you get lost in your own house?"

Ursula was just as puzzled as him, and suddenly launched herself through the door she *knew* was the correct one. Not so. *This* passageway took them to the Great Hall where they again stopped.

"It's as if the house is consciously taking us away from

173

where we *want* to be," Ursula said slowly, through a deeply annoyed frown. She clenched both fists so tightly that her knuckles lost all colour, and stared fixedly and very determinedly at the picture wall. So strong was her annoyance and so deep her concentrated inner strength, the Great Hall gave way to the recess in front of her father's study. Immediately it became solid, they both experienced the tingle, and as she reached out to touch the door *their* world evaporated. It was replaced by a moonlight-flooded world of thatched mud huts and glinting water. Jimmy recognised the Chieftain's Halls immediately. He grabbed Ursula's hand to move towards it, and noticed everyone stopped what they were doing and turn slowly towards them. They recognised Jimmy straight away and although they did not know who *she* was, they felt Ursula's hidden power, bowing low and shielding their faces from it as it passed. They slowed to a standstill, their movements frozen in time.

Several things happened virtually simultaneously. The Chieftain's Halls grew around Jimmy, the people were released from their inactivity, and Ursula disappeared. All light from the waxing moon had been veiled, as the gloom in the Hall deepened, to cut out everything except for the faint glow and swirling haze surrounding the Chieftain's chair. The room, like some hazy smoke-filled bar after closing time, was empty; except for the Chair. *That*, as ever, was occupied. As it could by right, be occupied by the Chieftain alone, *he* was in residence. Jimmy recognised the shape of the head, the mane of hair and the aura surrounding him. He approached slowly, carefully, so as not to irritate the great man. As Jimmy neared the chair its occupant turned, slowly, deliberately, anticipating the newcomer's actions.

"Chieftain," Jimmy said gravely, and as he did so he caught the glint of the eyes behind the bush of facial hair. "Is it Tarna? It can't be you! Are you now the Chieftain of Omni?"

"Tommy?" Tarna's brow furrowed at the mention of the name. "I knew you would come back sooner or later. I am sorry you had to return in such inauspicious times."

"It's Jimmy, Tommy's brother. Are you the Chieftain now?" Jimmy asked rather pointedly, knowing already that he couldn't be Chieftain unless he was a direct descendant; unless…the rightful heirs were all dead!

Tarna, the Chieftain of All Omni, fixed Jimmy with an aggressive glare, which all but silenced him verbally if not mentally. As Tarna didn't know much about Jimmy other than what Tommy had told him a long time before, he couldn't have accounted for his growth in mental faculty since the last time he was in Omni, and that he was beginning to develop his own powers.

"*I* am the Chieftain of All Omni," Tarna boomed rather grandly, "and I have no need to justify my position to you!"

Immediately, Jimmy was suspicious because the Tarna he had known about from his brother and Dominic would not have delivered such a pompous and arrogant speech. He felt something wasn't right.

The assumed smile behind the glower reasserted itself as Tarna spoke, in sugary tones this time.

"Jimmy," he oozed, "how good to see you. I hope you have brought good tidings with you. As you can no doubt see we have had a difficult time of late. How is your brother? Is he with you?"

"I know we left somewhat hastily in the middle of a battle last time we were here," Jimmy answered, "but I had no idea things might be as bad as this. Has Seth become too powerful?"

"A slight set-back, that's all." Tarna said, glossing over the obvious poor state of the land. "He will be defeated 'ere long. Then I, we, will take back what we have lost."

"What about Por and the Wandering People? Are they still here?" Jimmy asked. "And what of the Old Man of the Mountains? We saw him before we left last time." He did not let him know about Ursula or their meeting with her grandfather. He did not trust him now.

"Not been seen for a long time," he replied with a grand gesture. "Word has it that he has diminished to an old powerless hermit in the wild or he is, quite simply, dead." Jimmy remained silent throughout the diatribe, not letting Tarna see that he didn't believe this explanation.

"You must be in need of refreshment," he continued, clapping his hands to summon an aide. "Jaffed here will see to your needs."

With the arrival of this man, Jimmy was effectively dismissed and led away from his presence. The last he saw of Tarna was the back of his head wreathed in a blue swirling haze, rather like a tobacco smoker framed by a wreath of shifting pipe smoke. Fortunately, Jaffed had gotten to know Tommy quite well during the times he had been here before, and so Jimmy hoped he might glean information about the situation here now.

"How are things here *really*?" Jimmy asked Jaffed tentatively, understanding that he would need to be careful with his wording. "Things don't seem to be quite as good as before. " He paused to take in a little food – fruit, bread, and fruit juice – but Jaffed said little other than to speak of their situation in generalised terms. "I know the Old Man of the Mountains isn't dead. I've seen him, spoken to him, know he's not as lame and useless as perhaps might have been thought." The look of utter surprise on Jaffed's face told Jimmy that he had scored a direct hit.

"Come with me," Jaffed urged Jimmy, taking him by the elbow and leading him out of the Chieftain's hut. "We need to be somewhere we can't be overheard."

They entered a small hut on the southern-most edge of the village, a little detached from the others. They weren't seen as it was still dark outside, with a few clouds venturing inland and periodically obliterating the moon's pale glimmer. Once inside, Jaffed lit a small oil lamp which cast only enough of a glow to allow them both to see each other's facial features.

"The Chieftain of old suffered several serious defeats, both military and personal, at the hands of Seth," he started. "At first we all put it down to misfortune but these defeats became a little too regular. There is no way Seth could have inflicted all of that without internal help of some sort. We had our suspicions but could not prove who the informer might be, until one moonless night several weeks ago. We witnessed the most intense and prolonged battle of wills between the Chieftain and, we assumed, Seth. The struggle lasted an age, with great lightening storms raging in and around the Chieftain's hut, and we could do nothing but watch helplessly.

In the midst of one particularly violent onslaught, all activity ceased suddenly. We rushed into the hut to see what help we might give, but the Chieftain – our *proper* Chieftain – was no longer there. He had disappeared entirely. However, filling his Chair, as if he had a *right* to be there was Tarna. He was changed in a way we hadn't noticed before, much as you saw him today. He simply *assumed* the role of Chieftain, and nobody has dared to challenge him, not even the Chieftain's sons. As I said, we all have our suspicions and fears; all, that is, save those who support him and provide him with whatever counsel he *wants* to hear. Tarna never used to be *that* arrogant and self-opinionated."

Jaffed tailed off into a pensive silence, which lasted for several minutes, until Jimmy asked quite pointedly and unexpectedly, "What about Por and the Wandering People? Tarna didn't answer when I asked him earlier. And Algan, what about him?"

"I know nothing about any of these people," Jaffed faltered, after a moment's thought. It was as if he had never heard those names before. Or as if he realised suddenly he had said too much.

Intuitively Jimmy felt that, although his mental abilities had recently become heightened, Jaffed was able to shield the truth from him. A feeling of helplessness began to grow in his head, making him wonder if the Omni he had known was slipping away gradually, to be replaced by a world of deceit and evil.

Chapter Nineteen

Black dark. No light save the pale electric blue caught on the titanium edge of an ultra-sharp sword; craftsman built; hard as hell; no quarter. Where on earth is this place? This is no place on Earth! The black recedes slightly, only enough to allow the sighted to discern to whom they are speaking. The powerful amongst them have no need to see.

"Lore Masters!" came a low voice, all the while growing, like a dull throb in the head. "Lore Masters, show your skill to me. Bring me what I need to know, and you shall be exalted to the highest of the high. Fail me, and your fall shall be so low that it will depart this world forever, along with your entire line."

"Lord!" they chorused almost in unison.

They knelt, heads bowed, not daring to behold the countenance whence came these words of awe. They awaited his will with trepidation and dread. How was his mood? Would he favour or destroy them? The light waxed slightly to reveal an ebony throne set upon a black dais. Upon that throne sat a being of such power that no-one dared gaze upon its ever shifting, swirling, changing indistinct form. The fount of all evil, the pit from which all despair emanates, this was the Lord of Seth, once known as Tar-igor, brother to Gor-ifan from whom he wrested power so long ago.

"From your furthest memories and your most profound lore writings," he continued, "I need to know the deepest and most ancient evil ever to walk this world, and I must know now where it resides."

The faces of the six lore masters, acknowledged to be the most learned in the land, betrayed their dismay for they knew of no such entity, no evil deeper than that of the Seth himself. Yet, how could you find the way to tell him this when he had the power to snuff out your life force simply by thinking it? So they remained in pained and uncomfortable silence, hoping he would tire and release them. No such relief was to be their salvation. He must have the knowledge so that alliances might be struck and resistance to his plans removed.

"Well?" he boomed, taking voice once again.

"My Lord," stammered Albor, the one considered to be chief amongst them, "we don't …"

"There is one," a shrill voice rose through the deafening silence left by his superiors, "whom you seek."

"No, there..." faltered Albor.

"Silence!" Seth interrupted. "Let him speak. Who are you? Come forward."

Albor fell forward with a pained and strangled cry, and as the newcomer strode over his prostrate, cloaked body, the cloak became still and empty. Albor was no more.

A small dwarf-like figure stood before the dais, body straight and unbowed, his curiously sightless face unmoved by the majesty of his Lord before him. "My name is Untur, son of Untar, greatest lore master of this world. I am servant to the almighty Lord of Seth."

"Speak!" Seth ordered, unmoved by Untur's rhetoric. "Now!"

"Majesty," Untur continued, unabashed. "There is one considered long ago to be the ultimate evil power in this land. He was defeated and diminished one thousand ages of man ago by an alliance forged between this world and another, and imprisoned in the Crystal Realm whence there is no escape. He is called Umbrano, and I know how you might release him from his nether world prison."

A silence of such utter profundity fell over the gathering, that the blinking of an eyelash and the beating of the smallest heart could have caused such cacophony as to result in shock waves capable of throwing down trees and buildings.

"Where is this "Crystal Realm"?" Seth finally broke the silence with words, which crashed into the gathered listeners. "Is it to be found in this world?"

"It is not, my Liege," Untur responded with equal assurance. "It is not of any *physical* world. It can be found only by one powerful enough in mind and sorcery to unlock its secrets with a key whose whereabouts *I* have discovered."

"And where is this … this key that only you have access to, oh wisest and most learned lore master?" This he delivered with a powerful and crushing sarcasm, which had no effect at all on Untur. He simply stood his ground before the great sorcerer and prepared to deliver his answer with a self-confidence verging on arrogance. Who was this little-known dwarf and how had he come by such vital and telling information?

"I will take you through the secrets my father would have taken to his grave had I not intercepted his last thoughts," Untur began, unabashed. "However, I must have certain assurances that *I* will benefit from this alliance we are about to share."

"Assurances? Alliance?" Seth exploded. This outburst was designed to show all present that he did not brook minions lightly, and that *he*, the Seth, was in control, not some upstart dwarf. He *had* decided before Untur's declaration of "terms" that he would reward him as there was something about his arrogant, confident attitude, which he liked. If he proved to be as good as his word, *he* would be Seth's next chief lore master. Untur, recognising Seth's ploy, allowed him to win the attention and belief of all onlookers. *He* simply dipped his chin in an overt act of contrition and supplication. They both understood each other and the rules of engagement perfectly. Theirs would be an alliance to keep the balance of power firmly with the Lord of Evil.

"Your story *will* be of use to me and clear in its instruction," warned Seth, the menace in his voice growing clearly, "or you will share your former master's fate."

Untur inclined his head slightly to acknowledge the perilous agreement upon which he had set his seal, and in which he would not, could not, fail.

"The Crystal Realm is an invisible prison," Untur started, slowly choosing his words with great care, "which exists only in an alternate reality where those trapped exist behind crystal walls of an impenetrable strength, and which cannot be breached by force or guile. Not even the great and glorious Lord of Seth possesses the power to achieve this." He paused to cast a brief glance at his master, who was unmoved, intent, concentrating, eyes half-closed as if almost asleep. No response; no reaction. 'Was this a good sign?' he thought.

Untur continued, "The Realm was established, created by an alliance of four great forces, one thousand ages of man ago. Their joint powers forced Umbrano into it to spend the rest of eternity as a 'reward' for his attempt to conquer the world. They were the bearers of names some of which you will no doubt recognise – Algan of the Enchanted Forest, Ben-ruhe the Otherworldling, the Chieftain of All Omni, and your brother, Gor-ifan. I have an overwhelming feeling that none of them would agree to Umbrano's release, should you ask.

"The only alternative key is through the mind and spirit of a truly innocent young being from another world who enters *this* world of free will. This being has to be the chosen one with a strong link to the ancient order, and must be pure of mind and heart. I feel sure the great and glorious Lord of Seth will know such a being."

"Indeed I do," Seth's response came, after a few moments thought. "There is one whose arrival in this world visited a major disruption to my plans. He it was who became the unsought catalyst for the forging of an alliance between the disparate riff-raff peoples of this world against me. He it was who was instrumental in the release of my niece Miriel from my care, and the rousing of my archenemy, Algan, from his rustic slumbers. He is the focus of all our wrath, and must be taken even more urgently now to further our cause. He is named Jimmy Scoggins, and we believe he is here in this world now."

The room had grown progressively darker the more intense Seth's pronouncements had become, with lightening playing around his ever increasing temples.

Without warning, he was gone, the audience was over, and the lore masters gathered, unsure, outside the audience chamber. Untur somehow found himself in the midst of a loose circle of ancient lore masters, shuffling towards him in as menacing a fashion as lore masters feel able. Untur, unrepentant and un-cowed, raised himself to his full dwarfish height, held his head up and raised his hand to them in quasi-friendly warning. Recognising that, perhaps, he was a force not to be trifled with, they backed away and disappeared into the darkness.

Untur remained, entirely alone, enjoying the feeling of elation which success had heralded. He *would* be the Chief Lore Master, of that he was sure. He was also sure, at some time in the not-too-distant future, he would have a much more crucial role to play in the ordering of this realm.

"Not good!" Jimmy thought. "Not good!" He wasn't at all sure how he was going to escape this situation, where nothing he saw was as it should have been. Tarna was not to be trusted and Jaffed had lied. How many more of these people, he had known of and called friends, were not now true to their shared ideals. He felt he had to find the Wandering People somehow, or make his way to Oompah's castle, where he hoped he might find truth and clarity. What he would have given for a number 59 bus!

The black of night was already beginning to give way to the grey of early morning as dawn signalled its approach. But what was he about to see in this now unsure and unsafe place? Previously he would have beheld many dun-coloured huts hugging the lush green grassland, fastened about by a silver ribbon of bright water that was the River Lin. Already in the half-light he could make out that there were fewer dwellings, some in ruins and some flattened completely. He felt tired, more so than he had ever felt before, and he wanted to be home. The thing about adventures was that they were great on a full stomach and first thing on a bright summer's morning. Late autumn with a setting chill, no sleep, and an empty belly didn't do it for Jimmy at all.

On his first visit he would have been offered rest, shelter and sustenance in one of the friendly dwellings hereabouts. Now it might have been an alien village, where a body could perish without anyone taking too much notice. And fear; there was the overwhelming scent of fear in the air, which was strengthened by a liberal dose of uncertainty and confusion. Would anyone offer him sanctuary or, better still, help and advice as to which way to go?

"You are the Otherworldling Scoggins," a deeply guttural voice jolted him out of his thoughts. Jimmy spun on his heels to see a gathering group of villagers he had not seen before. They were swarthy and bore none of the characteristics of the people he had met in Omni before. Although Jimmy was now only ten, he had built up a sophisticated value system in his short time and so he recognised antagonism and aggression when he saw it. The group approaching him was not a welcoming gathering and they were not about to offer him succour.

"You are not welcome here!" the leader growled, "and we have ways of making sure you do not return." They shambled slowly towards him in an alarmingly threatening way, obliging Jimmy to retreat as quickly as he could without running – just yet. He knew by their demeanour that discussion about the finer points of friendliness and hospitality would be futile, so he turned rapidly on his heels once again and took flight. Only three paces into his escape, he bounced off a wall of muscle and sinew, as villagers from the other side of the river closed in, to be gripped by a pair of hairy, muscular hands on his rebound. At that moment, a high piercing screech rose sharply into the air, to be answered almost immediately by another somewhere the other side of the village.

Jimmy screwed his eyes tight shut as if trying to wish away a nasty dream, knowing in his heart that Seth wouldn't let him escape a second time. He screwed himself up even tighter, expecting the inevitable. When nothing happened to him for several minutes, he unclenched his fists and unscrewed his nerves, to have the hissing and screaming in his ears replaced by – silence, and a slowly increasing wheeze. Now *that* sound he *had* heard before. One eye gradually opened to reveal – blackness. The other eye joined the first to show – even blacker blackness, turning slowly to deep grey.

"The Foggy Land of Four!" he groaned. "Have I escaped *that* fate to be thrust into *this* one?" His companions, the owner of the hairy arms and the one to whom the acrid and nauseous smell of stale, unwashed sweat, had let go of their prisoner to become captive themselves. *They* would become Whispering People along with countless others trapped here. Jimmy screwed his eyes again, and immediately felt a sharp corner in the small of his back and the smell of baking in his nostrils. The intense light of a bright autumn day almost blinded him as he opened his eyes again to be greeted by Ursula's concerned face, not two metres from his as he sprawled against a kitchen unit in her house.

She made a lurch for him to keep him there but to no avail. The kitchen unit was replaced by something infinitely larger and considerably harder. He had landed amidst the legs of Por's Imperial Guard, with his face squashed against a giant kneecap. He had hoped to remain in the kitchen at Ursula's house, where the smell of baking had caused his stomach to lurch in anticipation, but the Imperial Guard in his situation was a close second best. At least he would not be attacked by crazed Seth supporters and followers.

"Well!" Por, the King of the Wandering People said at last, once Jimmy had been placed upright and taken to his audience. "We meet again young master Scoggins. I can see you are in need of sustenance once more, which is fortuitous as we are about to dine. Please join us."

Those words "dine" and "join us" had become Jimmy's favourites in a world where he never knew where or whence his next meal might arrive, so he had learned to fill his belly as full as he might without bursting. This he set to doing with a vengeance. Por had recalled his appetite from the last time they had met, and so allowed him to finish before plying him with the inevitable questions, "Where did you come from? Why here, and why now? Who are you trying to escape from?"

"I need to see Oompah as a matter of some importance," Jimmy urged Por after he had dined. The usual fare was more than enough to satisfy his empty belly, which now, of course, was as full as he could have made it.

"I have learned," Por began his slow reply, "to listen seriously to your pronouncements however crazy they may sound. And here you are once again, appearing unsought for in my land at a time of great strife and need. You are beginning to acquire the reputation as something of a harbinger of doom and dismay. Why do you need to see His Majesty Oompah?"

"I don't know whether I ought to tell *him* this before I tell you," Jimmy replied seriously, "but here goes …" and with this, he launched into his experience with Tarna and the villagers. Once he had finished his story, Por sat in deep and brooding silence for several long minutes, brow furrowed and shoulders hunched.

"This does not come as a complete surprise to me," Por answered finally. "We have had concerns about his people for quite some time and we had heard rumours about the true Chieftain's disappearance. The news about Tarna, however, is a shock. Relations between our peoples had always been convivial and robust, until the shadow from the north had begun to stretch its icy fingers towards us. We are on our way to our western realm and will escort you towards Oompah's castle beyond Lake Soon. We should be there by mid-day tomorrow so you need to rest now."

Rest was a luxury Jimmy had not experienced much lately, and the idea of rest whilst travelling Wandering People-style appealed to him enormously. The problem was that this sort of rest, although refreshing and invigorating in the extreme, didn't *seem* to last long; no sooner asleep, than being woken at the end of the journey. This was their fashion, and so it was that "moments" after Jimmy had settled he was being awoken, close to the southern-most shore of Lake Soon.

"Here we must bid farewell," Por said to Jimmy, as the Wandering People prepared to strike out south and west.

"We have prepared further rations for you so that you will be sustained until you reach Oompah's castle. Fare well until ..."

The trap snapped shut! The Wandering People had not expected to be ambushed by such a large force, laying in wait so quietly and patiently, with such targeted precision. They were always ready for such an attack, but three of the Imperial Guard soon lay on the ground around Por, with black-feathered arrows sprouting from their sides. They would not die but would be incapacitated for a while.

A blaring of brazen trumpets signalled a further attack from the right flank from man-high creatures clad in black breastplates and ghoulishly fashioned helmets. By this time, the remaining Guard had formed a tight ring around their king and would neither yield nor break rank. *They* would not allow their king to be harmed! They left sufficient space between each Guardsman to allow swing and slash of their mighty swords, which they used to devastating effect. The rest of the Wandering People fought like demons, decimating the enemy forces as they cleaved through their ranks. That was the effect Seth's forces had planned for, for indeed it was the Lord of Evil who had designed the diversion. Jimmy was left in the open, an unguarded ten year old in the midst of a raging battle of hardened and seasoned warriors each more than twice his height. This was not good, Jimmy thought once again. At its fiercest the battle raged, ploughing over heaps of dead and wounded, when a small group of enemy warriors broke away from the skirmish they were involved with, and headed for the unguarded and unprotected youngster. He turned to flee but ran into a wall of sinew and bone closing in from the other side. A strong bony hand clamped itself painfully around his upper arm, and another silenced the cry in his throat. He was taken!

At that moment, a terrible and terrifying crash of thunder and flash of bright blinding blue light split the air. The two groups of would-be captors lay at Jimmy's feet scorched beyond recognition. All hostilities ceased in that one instant with most of the enemy forces either dead or in rout. The Guard and all the Wandering People simply stood, frozen in action, mouths open in disbelief. For, on one small hillock in the middle of where the hottest battle had raged, stood the diminutive figure of a slight, raven-haired girl, her right hand held above her head, palm outward in warning. A power of significant intensity, which this age of Omni had never witnessed, emanated from her to a great distance around and beyond her. Four enemy warriors made a last desperate lurch to capture their goal but were utterly destroyed by this young girl. They were crushed as an elephant stepping on a small insect.

It was Ursula, and no sooner had she appeared than she had gone.

With only a few injuries and no fatalities, Por viewed the attack as a mere skirmish in his terms. However, the mind-blowing intervention of one so small, wielding seemingly limitless power, was entirely a different matter.

"That level of power we have never seen before," he said to his gathered elders, "not even from Algan of the Enchanted Forest. She is not of this world either."

"It was prophesied that such an infant would appear," replied Feisor, his chief adviser and elder. "That time is at hand. We must find where it is and …"

"Hang on a minute," interrupted Jimmy. "If you don't mind, the 'it' you are talking about is my friend, and she's called Ursula."

The king and his advisers stopped their discussion and turned slowly to face the source of their interruption.

"You were not invited to this discussion," Por said quietly but with authority. "However, seeing as you *are* here, perhaps you might like to help us to find your friend?"

"She's not here," Jimmy replied, "and I'm not sure she'd come if you asked. Besides, *I* would like to see King Oompah, and we're not quite there yet."

"As a matter of fact," continued Feisor, "if you look over your left shoulder, you'll see …"

"Oompah's castle," Jimmy continued under his breath, following his direction.   With that, he struck out towards the drawbridge linking the castle to the mainland. The castle hadn't changed at all, or so he thought, but it was a while since he was last here. Nonetheless, it felt strange stepping onto the solid bridge. Solid bridge? Shouldn't he have felt springy planking under his feet? This didn't feel right …

Immediately that thought took shape in his head the light went out, blackness took over, to be followed almost instantly by a swirling snow effect; the sort of effect you get when a TV goes off station. The only difference was that this *was* snow, real snow, and with the snow came a keen, bitingly cold north wind, which whistled through his clothes as if he had nothing on at all.

To Por, the Wandering People and all other onlookers, Oompah's castle simply disappeared and Jimmy along with it. This was immediately replaced by − Oompah's castle! The one Jimmy had stepped into had been an illusion, an exceedingly clever and realistic projection from the mind of the master of deception. He was taken once more, and this time there would be no escape.

Coming soon...

Magic Parcel: The Gathering Storm

Want to find out what happens to Jimmy in the next instalment of the Magic Parcel series?

Well this is a dilemma and no mistake! How is Jimmy going to escape this one? Miriel helped him and his brother escape when Seth caught them in their last adventure, but there's no one to save Jimmy this time, except, perhaps, for Ursula. *She* is determined that her new friend will not become a lost friend.

She has shown flashes of her raw and unrefined power already, but how can she save Jimmy if she can't find *him* or control her new found talents? What would happen if she unleashed her power in its full force now?

Jimmy and Ursula are Otherworldlings, and not the only ones needing help in Omni. How would ordinary (and extra-ordinary) Omnians react to the emergence of a new and potentially more destructive threat, not only to their stability but also to their very existence? Is the answer in Omni itself, or in some other place?

Find out in Frank's thrilling sequel, coming soon!

Updates and more information can be found about 'The Gathering Storm' at www.frankenglish.co.uk

About the author - Frank English

Born in 1946 in the West Riding of Yorkshire's coalfields around Wakefield, he attended grammar school where he enjoyed sport rather more than academic work. After three years at teacher training college in Leeds, Frank became a teacher in 1967. He spent a lot of time during his teaching career entertaining children of all ages, a large part of which was through telling stories, and encouraging them to escape into a world of imagination and wonder. He found some of his most troubled youngsters to be very talented poets. Frank has always had a wicked sense of humour, which has blossomed during the time he has spent with his present wife. This sense of humour also allowed many youngsters to survive often difficult and upsetting home environments.

Recently, Frank retired after forty years working in schools with young people, most of whom had significantly disrupted lives due to behavioural disorders and poor social environments, generally brought about through circumstances beyond their control. At the same time as moving from leafy lane suburban middle class school teaching to residential schooling for the emotional and behavioural disturbed in the early 1990s, divorce provided the spur to achieve ambitions. Supported by his present wife, Denise, he achieved a Master's degree in his mid-forties and a PhD at the age of fifty-six, something he had always wanted to do.

Now enjoying glorious retirement, Frank spends as much time as life will allow writing, reading and travelling.